I0517576

EVIL GROWS IN THE DARK

A SHORT STORY COLLECTION

KENT SHAWN

Join the Kent Shawn Newsletter of Doom for book giveaways free content advanced access to new books and exclusive behind the scenes material.

https://www.kentshawn.com/newsletter/

J esse stood at the entrance to a white room.

"Please come in and have a seat, Mr. Callum." Her name tag read *Ms. Bernice Federal Health Care Tech Grade I.* She was an adjuster, clean and neat to the point of the surreal. Her plain white clothes matched the clinic's walls, dimly luminescent and without seams.

"I'm not sure why I'm here," Jesse said, trying to keep the edge from his voice and in no hurry to enter the blank room and float in white oblivion. "It's only a headache, and I have work."

Ms. Bernice smiled and waited, pleasant and implacable. Jesse surrendered and sat in the room's only furnishing. An oval contour alignment chair, also sterile white. The Inner-link portal at his wrist glowed blue, offering some much-needed color. It transmitted sense data to the chair, and the seat molded itself to Jesse with a hiss of air.

"Did the link-trace have a diagnosis? Am I getting an adjustment?"

"I didn't read the trace, Mr. Callum, but relax. We are the best clinic in Tennessee, you will be back to work in no time."

Jesse nodded and gave her a weak smile. The Nashville clinic was big and state of the art, the first universal clinics on the coasts were falling apart. He held out his wrist, the blue diamond of his portal glowing softly, ready to link and get this over with.

"No, no," Ms. Bernice said, "I am not your tech today. He is on his way. Just relax and enjoy the wall."

"You sure you don't know what this is about?"

Ms. Bernice paused at the door. "I am sure the Director will answer all your questions. Please try and relax, Mr. Callum—we are here to help."

Jesse swallowed a cold hunk of fear. Sweat bloomed on his forehead. "Thanks."

Ms. Bernice waved her wrist across a panel in the white wall. It glowed blue in answer to her portal. The door slid shut behind her, slick and silent. Jesse bet his portal would not open that door.

Jesse's wife Erin had come to this clinic six years ago. Maybe to this same room. That year had been a whirlwind, freshly minted doctorates on the wall, hers in botany, his in engineering. Jesse's Doctorate thesis had landed him a job as a project manager for Innerlink to all his peers' envy. Then fate swung twin hammers down to smash their lives. Jesse confessed his secret desire. Then Erin got sick.

I am. I think.

His head did hurt, a circular throb near his temples, like a schoolyard bully's thumbs pressing in. He had never heard of a headache precipitating a healthcare call-in. Jesse squirmed in the comfortable chair. Unwilling to bear the unrelieved white any longer, Jesse thought: *Wall on.* His portal flashed blue, and the wall flared to life. Floor to ceiling white clouds drifted by on a field of deep blue, a standard three dimensional for a rest screen.

Jesse thought: *News.*

The drifting clouds were replaced by the stern face of Taylor Nelson, the self-proclaimed voice of America.

"Terrorists attacked a healthcare clinic in Seattle today, claiming the lives of three federal workers. Healthcare techs, both grade I, Teresa Wiley, Jeremy Evens, and the facility Director, Edmond Graham. The criminal, or criminals, escaped without being seen, and no link-trace was established. This brutal attack is the sixth of the so-called *ghost* phenomenon. Our hearts go out to the families and friends of the deceased."

The newscast cut to a shot of a burning building, an older model universal clinic. It was a grey aging shadow compared to the modern monstrosity in which Jesse was currently ensconced. Chemical sprays suffocated the flames. Through the white foamy streams, defacing the Federal Board of Health and Wellness motto, '*We are here to help,*' a name was scrawled in livid red.

Jesse thought: *Wall off.*

The wall flickered, the image suspended, the red name hung like a shout. Then the wall went white.

I am. I think.

Jesse's heart pounded out stroke rhythms. He took deep breaths and tried to slow it down, wiping clammy palms on his slacks. They were probably monitoring his vitals through his link. They might get suspicious. People did not get this worked for adjustments. Thousands received them every day. What happened to Erin was a fluke. *It was my fault.*

When you jerk the wheel of your car going eighty, you were bound to crash. That's what Jesse had done to their lives the night he told Erin his fantasy.

"Have you ever thought about kids?" Jesse asked as they snuggled in bed, the lights dimmed, the wall pitched low.

Erin laughed. "Right, I spent the last eight years in college to quit and play mommy."

That stung. Jesse tried to hide it, but his body betrayed him. She turned to face him, brushing black hair aside, surprise, and a species of humor on her face.

"Oh, God, your serious." She lay a hand on his chest as if to read his heart.

"I was just thinking out loud."

"Children," she said in a small voice. Her eyes drifted. Erin's mind was made up before the last syllable left her lips. She had taken the first step toward her death.

A chime sounded. The door's control panel glowed red. A control link. A Director. The door hissed open, and a man walked in. He was middle-aged, tall, and on the way to fat. Unlike the other employees at the clinic in their seamless white, he wore a rumpled Hawaiian shirt in sickening pinks and purples, untucked, shirttail lounging over white jeans. Flip flops on hairy feet. The scruff of beard on his face looked five days old, and he beamed at Jesse from under sun-bleached bangs in need of a cut.

"Hi Jesse, I'm Cary." He gave his name tag a tap, it said Cary Evans and that was all. At each wrist, a portal glowed red, hexagonal instead of diamond. Only Directors had those portals. He waved an arm, seemingly at random, and a section of wall parted. A second chair slid out on a cushion of air. "Mind if I sit?"

Jesse mumbled, "Sure, free country."

Evans flopped into the chair; one leg flung over the side. "How are you feeling, Jesse?"

"I have a pretty good headache. Wouldn't have thought it was enough for a call-in. My portal needs service, could be that."

"You need service, a link engineer?" Evans laughed. "If you can't get service, what are us regular folks to do?"

This guy was far from regular folks, his eye twitched. Jesse suspected he had juiced up his neural rig. Overclocking was dangerous, some minds cracked under the strain.

The silence stretched out between them, Evans smiling, Jesse sweating.

At last, Evans sniffed and went on. "So, you're working at Innerlink, project manager for Cradle Sync. We are quite the important dude, aren't we, Jesse?"

Jesse ground his teeth at the mention of Cradle Sync. "I don't want to be rude, but if I am here on a health care call-in, can we get on with it? I have work."

"Nothing is more important than your health, brother. Relax, we are here to help." Evans leaned forward, brushing tawny hair back from wide eyes. "You know what a Director *does*? I bet a link engineer has a pretty good idea."

"I know about your link system."

"Come on, Jesse, don't be shy, you've heard the stories— all garbage, but I want to know what you think."

I think you erase people that cause trouble. I think you delete the parts of them that are hard to control, and a happy puppet walks out of this white hell of a clinic.

"You're here to help me?" Jesse said.

"Bingo! Jesse scores. Hope you mean that." Evans gave him a sly grin. "Not just having a little fun with Cary, right?"

Jesse sketched a laugh and stopped himself short from wiping the cold sweat from his forehead. Walking out of this room, the same man, was a proposition he could feel slipping away—all for the name on the brick wall. The name scrawled in red.

I am. I think

"Let's get to it, Jesse. You ready?" Flipping back his long

bangs, he investigated the portal on his right wrist. A cone of light splashed up a few inches above his forearm, forming a three-dimensional screen in livid red. Characters and colors sped by, Evan's eyes locked open painfully wide and unblinking as data flowed past faster than Jesse could follow.

This guy is overclocked by at least ten. He'll burn himself out if he keeps this up.

The red screen winked out, and the portal went dark. "Your file says you have never been adjusted." Evan's eyes narrowed from bulging insanity back to something approximating normal. "You've got to tell me your secret, bro. Never sick enough to need medicine, no broken bones, not even a stitch. You must have an angel on your shoulder."

"Just lucky, I guess."

"Damn lucky."

Jesse understood his confusion. The Innerlink system was a nano-bot constructed neural net that ran up the spine and connected with the brain. Within six months of your first injection, you were wired. Their labors finished; the Nano-bots went dormant.

Transport, household controls, and internal cellular comms were now all run by thought and wrist portal. Like the smart-phone revolution in early 2000, Innerlink took the world by storm. A person could think an electronic funds transfer or whisper a message in a friend's ear half the world away. No one got lost anymore. Links automatically sent messages to first responders if the host was in distress. There was always someone there to help.

"It makes me wonder, Jesse? Have you *really* never been sick? Or did your big ole' engineer brain figured a way around health care call-ins?"

"Obviously not, I'm here."

The Federal Total Wellness Act, arguably the most

disputed piece of legislation ever passed, allowed the Federal Board of Health and Wellness to use the links to monitor all enrollees' health. Factory updates to link systems now included sophisticated biomonitoring. Coming down with tonsillitis? You got a call-in. Cancers that previously went undiagnosed were treated at the onset. Countless lives were prolonged and saved. The program flourished; the opposition faded. Soon the Federal Program was the primary health care provider for 98% of the populace. The other two percent used knives on their kitchen tables.

By the time Jesse got his job at Innerlink, the sixth amendment to the original FTWA had slipped in silently under the radar. It became known as the "Adjustment Act." Knowledge of the amendment sifted its way into the public consciousness. The amendment allowed for anyone with a health care call-in that met the criteria stated under the law to undergo a "mental health adjustment." Most call-ins fit the requirements. At first, the adjustments targeted depression, anti-social, and compulsive behaviors. The flare of outrage subsided as friends and loved ones kicked addictions and stopped biting their nails.

Jesse knew about the adjustments and how they were made. There were soft adjustments and hard adjustments. The one that killed Erin was soft. Hers had been made by an adjuster like the clean seamless women that led Jesse to this chamber. Hard adjustments were more like deletions. Those could only be performed by Directors, like this smiling mess in front of him.

"So, Jesse, my man, headache, right?"

"Yes." *This smiling mess who thinks I'm a terrorist.*

"Are we getting enough sleep? Staying hydrated?" The corners of his mouth turned down, pulling at his eyes.

"Avoiding stressful situations?" Pregnant pause. "Having bad dreams?"

The Director's portals glowed red. Jesse's blue portal flared in answer. An unpleasant warmth ran through his arm and up and down his spine. A new spring of fresh sweat spouted to top the sour old.

We are linked now. The bastard is in my head. Oh, God...
I am, I think.

"I dream about my wife sometimes." Jesse's voice came out a dry croak.

"Your wife, so sad. So rare and tragic. A real kick to the balls, Jesse. Over five years now, right?"

"Almost six."

"How does a man ever get over a thing like that? We should have called you in, gave you an adjustment for the grief. I will say this, Erin must have been one clever girl. Most experts thought a linked suicide was impossible."

"Erin was the first."

"Enough to make a man angry, bitter?"

"Yes."

"Enough for him to look for someone to blame?"

The heat in Jesse's head grew to the point of pain. "I know what you want, but I can't help you."

"What do I want, Jesse?"

"I never met her. She contacted me."

"Who, Jesse?"

The heat increased. Pressure began to build behind Jesse's eyes. "Stop, you're hurting me."

"Who contacted you, Jesse?"

Jesse fell from the contour chair, knees cracking on the cold white floor. Head held in his hands, Jesse cried, "Please..."

Evans stood and loomed over him, bathed in the lurid

glow of his burning portals. "I am *tuning* you to feel pain from guilt, Jesse, feeling a little guilty?"

"Her name is..." the word would not come. But the pain did.

I am. I think.

"Yes?"

"Make it stop, God..." Jesse's words collapsed into a wounded cry.

"No?" Evan's toothsome grin split his face. "Then allow me." He spun like a dancer waving his wrist as he cavorted across the room. The chairs joined him in his dance, spinning, and hissing as they vanished into a wall compartment. Evans came to a stop, feet splayed. With a flourish fit for the circus, he brandished one wrist at Jesse, the other at the viewing wall.

The pain vanished, and the wall screen surged to life. Jesse slumped in relief. But on the wall, no fluffy clouds paraded by; no field of blue. Instead, it was a still image, the last moment of the newscast, a burning clinic, a red name. Magnified and focused in exquisite detail, runnels of paint ran from the sprayed letters like fresh blood.

LYDIA

Fighting back a sob—the pain unmanned him—Jesse's eyes locked on the bleeding name. His knees hurt against the cold hard floor, he wanted to stand, but his guts were like water.

I am. I think.

"Jesse, Jesse, Jesse..." Evans stalked in slow bouncing steps, circling like a buzzard with the first scent of death in its nose. "Do you like your job?"

"You have to let me explain..."

"Cuz, I love mine." Jared jumped down into a crouch, his nose an inch from Jesse's. "I get up every morning *fucking thrilled* to help people like you. That's what I live for, fixing all the ungrateful little fucks like you. I am *here* to help."

Jesse cowered back from the heat, cooking off Evan's face. The walls were tinted red from the frozen image on the viewer.

"And you brother, you—need—my—help. Your *health* is in jeopardy."

A thought shot through Jesse's head like a bullet, and hope ran out of the wound. *This guy has overclocked himself insane. Even if we weren't linked, he could probably tear my head off. No matter what I say, he will rummage around in my head, deleting until I am gone, and no one remembers Erin.*

"I like being a link engineer. I have nothing personal against Innerlink."

"Oh, that was a careful answer, Jesse." Evans resumed his circling. "Come on, what do you really think about Innerlink and the Federal Health and Wellness Act? I'm worried, Jesse. Did what happened to your wife open a door inside you that should stay closed in all—*healthy* citizens? That is all it takes. Just a crack." His smile evaporated, and his face flushed. "For a terrorist like Lydia to slither in."

"The adjustment didn't kill Erin. I did it when I told her I wanted kids. I don't blame anyone but myself."

I am. I think.

The same week Jesse told Erin he wanted children; she had a fertility test. All women were rendered sterile at puberty for over twenty years when Erin came of age. It was a simple process and reversible. They had almost burst with happiness when the test came back clean. She had none of the two hundred or so undesirable characteristics that precluded a woman from a procreation license. Within the month, she had a life inside her.

Erin wanted a girl. Jesse didn't argue. They selected a

female of middle height, with a generous division of features between mother and father and crossed their fingers. Sex assignment was simple but getting the mother's dimples and father's hair might go either way.

Jesse was up to his ears, pitching the Cradle Sync project. Nano-bots installed in the womb achieved heightened synergism as the fetus's nervous system and the link's integration fibers developed together. The number of connections would increase by a power of ten, giving their link new access to the brain. Even the control links the Directors possessed could only sense and isolate emotions. Cradle sync would change the world forever.

"Imagine," Jesse would say to his coworkers, "Being able to think to your child in the womb. To share your feelings selectively and interactively with those you love. We could understand each other for the first time. Truly understand. Language would be no barrier."

Meanwhile, the Federal Health Directors were creating the first adjustment lists. They were also choosing Health Centers for testing: Nashville, Little Rock, Dallas. Everywhere the powers that be thought there was the most backward thinking. As Jesse was designing Cradle Sync, the first adjustments began.

Evans looked somber. "What happened to your wife was unfortunate, Jesse. But it wasn't anyone's fault." His portal flared, and his eyes bulged as flash traffic speed across the holographic screen. "Erin Callum got a nasty infection in her lungs, complications resulting in pneumonia, priority one due to pregnancy. Call in, medication, and standard mental health adjustment. Three months later, suicide."

Rage tore through Jesse like a talon. It left him bare for one sticky moment.

Evans, eyes still bulging, locked onto Jesse like some

predatory insect. "I felt that Jesse. I would be pissed off too. She should have never been given that set of adjustments. Not a pregnant woman. That protocol was still in the test phase."

Jesse's headache was really stomping now. "She should have never been pregnant at all." He tried to swallow the guilt and anger, both useless here. He could feel the tight awareness that was Director Evans inside his head. It was wary, on guard, like a coiled spring.

Evans extinguished his screen and resumed his circling. "So, you don't blame us for Erin's Death?"

"Looking at this place makes me sick. It doesn't make me a terrorist." Jesse was tired of being looked down on by this man but could not find the strength to rise. The floor was ice, but his head felt hot and wrapped in wool. The headache grew, the pain sharp.

"But Lydia contacted you just the same. What did she want, Jesse?"

"I know what you think. You think Lydia wanted a way to burn down clinics without being caught."

"Could someone *do* that with the Cradle Sync architecture, Jesse? Could they make ghosts who can't be tracked by their links?"

"No one knows what Cradle Sync can do yet. No one."

In the years since Erin's death, Jesse had taken to walking. It took an hour to walk home from his office. He needed that hour to ready himself to enter the house where he found her, hanging in the closet, dark hair obscuring her face, belly like swollen fruit.

One day, on the way home, a flash of red in an alley caught his eye. There was seldom graffiti in this day and age. It was easy as hell to get caught and impossible to run when the police could track your Innerlink system to within a meter. But there it was in red paint.

JESSE

Startled, Jesse looked around. The passersby ignored the red name, *his* name. They ignored him. Like he was a ghost. The next day it was gone. A month later, he saw red again.

YOU KNOW THEY KILLED HER

This time panic gripped him, and he fled. Who would play a cruel joke like this? Eventually, his anger dissolved into tears. He resolved to take the tube to work.

A week later, he walked home, but the alley was empty. Then he walked every day, sometimes even returning after sundown drawn by the empty brick wall.

The day he swore to abandon this obsession, he found red letters waiting for him.

LOOK FOR MY NAME

A few nights later, the first Federal Health Clinic burned, its Director murdered. No one had been seen, no link-trace made. The report flashed across the flickering wall, and Jesse fell from his chair in an ignoble sprawl, his dinner slopping onto the floor. The wall was filled with the familiar crimson scrawl.

LYDIA

Jesse's first thought was to report the strange messages. People were dead. He activated his portal to make the call, but something stopped him.

I am. I think.

Whoever Lydia was, she knew about Erin. She knew about him.

Evans had stopped his pacing. "Were there any more marks on the wall?"

"One more." Jesse felt drained. The memories pulsed and

throbbed in his head. "It read: *Find the list, and I will find you.*"

"Ah, the list. The first adjustment protocol that killed your wife." Evans nodded. "They wanted to turn you against your country, to get you to do nasty things for Lydia and her ghosts. You found it didn't you, Jesse?"

"It wasn't hard. My office makes sure the Innerlink hardware can support the software for adjustment protocols." Jesse tried to meet Evans' eyes. "I guess the powers that be thought we breed a little too often here in the middle USA." He was surprised how even he sounded. He had wept and raged the first dozen times he read the lines of suggestion that killed his wife and unborn daughter. He knew it word for word.

Jesse finally locked eyes with Evans, and in a steady voice, he let it spill out of him. The words stained the sterile room. "Having children is a burden on myself, those I love, and the society I live in. I will not be a burden."

"Yes, that was in the original batch," Evans said. "Still there, in a much better-written version. Your wife's case was instructive. The middle of the country had been voting against progress for thirty years. They had to be winnowed." Evans laughed. "Really, it was not the item on the adjustment list that went wrong. It was the delivery."

"What the hell does that mean—"

Evan's links both burned bright. A brief swimming vertigo engulfed Jesse. Then it was replaced by the overwhelming desire to bite into a raw ripe tomato. He could feel his teeth breaking the tense red skin and the squirt of the cold juices hitting the top of his mouth. The sensations faded, but the taste lingered.

Evans cackled as Jesse raised a finger to his lips. "Tomatoes are good for you, Jesse. There, your first adjustment, my man. If you had ever been sick and had a health care call-in, you would already be excited about a healthy diet. Would have added years to your life and saved the good old US of A a truckload of cash taking care of you in your later years."

"Erin didn't come home, craving tomatoes." The bitterness in his voice was in stark contrast with the sweet taste on his lips.

"No, no, she didn't. Those early adjustments were implanted through both positive and negative reinforcement. That, in hindsight, was a big mistake. Only the positive these days, Jesse. I didn't implant the suggestion that candy bars are disgusting. But guess what, if I offered you a Snickers bar or a vine-ripe tomato, you would pick the fruit every time. Forever. See—positive. The negative ones, well, they developed into negative behaviors."

When Erin came home from the very same clinic where her husband currently cowered on the floor, her infection was gone, and the baby slept safe inside her. All Jesse could talk about was their daughter. He begged Erin to consider being in the human trials for Cradle Sync. The beta test was already in chimps and functioning perfectly. They could *hear* their child think. Wasn't it exciting? How could she say no?

Erin gave short answers. She changed the subject. As their child's warm heart and mind grew inside her, so did a second darker child of confusion. *I will not be a burden.* Her adjustment bent her against herself. Her love for Jesse was the lever.

She left no note.

Jesse lost track of how long he had sat on the floor, sweating as the grinning bug-eyed monster circled him like a vulture. He wasn't sure how much more healthcare he could endure.

"What happens now?" Jesse was trembling and ashamed.

The headache had dulled, receded. He almost wished he had it back, to distract him from his loss and this white hell where he cowered before one of the architects of Erin's death.

Evans hunkered down in front of him, eyes glittering. "What now? I'll tell you what now. You tell me everything you know about Lydia. She has killed three Directors with her 'Ghosts.'" He imbued the word Director with an almost religious reverence. "The Police are worthless now; without a link-trace they couldn't find a jaywalker, much less a terrorist. Did you do it, Jesse? Who else but a link engineer *could* teach them to shut down the tracker on their link system? Who else but a bereaved hubby and daddy *would*? We have technicians trying to duplicate the feat, but everyone has failed."

Jesse was silent. This had always been why he was here.

"Remember, Jesse, I am listening in that head of yours. Not mind reading, like your Cradle Sync promises, but I am damn good at it. If I sense you are holding something back, well, that's where the fun begins. You thought my guilt-heat trick was a bummer. I can light every pain receptor in your body like little candles. Think you can take the pain? I can take your memories. I won't know exactly what they are, Jesse, but I have learned to know the good from the bad. I'll find the best and squeeze till they pop. One by one, they'll go till you are barely human at all. Never to remember your first kiss or your mother's love. No moments of triumph that shaped you into a man. How about a lifetime of education snipped in random places, leaving you a sad, confused creature? I can do it all."

I am. I think.

"How do they do it, Jesse? How are they killing Directors? Anyone with my link system should have stopped them cold. And last but not least, the million-dollar question—how do I find Lydia?" Evan's grin became feral.

Jesse searched for courage. But in the bowels of the clinic that killed his wife, trapped in white oblivion with this madman who could kill him with a thought, it was like trying to grasp smoke. "I don't know where she is; she finds me and leaves me messages."

"We know that already, Jesse. There are only two or three engineers with your knowledge of all the new systems. A nan-injector with Cradle Sync went missing years ago, an empty delivery fluid in its place. Before that, no Ghosts."

"I didn't give anyone Cradle Sync I took it for—"

"For what, what did you do with it?" Evan's portals flared angry red. "Better answer quick. Give me what I want, or I will start taking things from you."

"I came home I found her hanging—"

"You're out of time, Jesse." The lurid glow of his portals made Evans ghoulish.

"Erin was still warm. If I had only got home a few minutes earlier— I could sense something crying out within her—broadcasting to my portal. Not words, but a thought so powerful, so *alive*.

I am. I think.

"What are you talking about?" Evan's expression slipped from its predatory grimace. Doubt crept forward.

"I opened my link to the signal. The thought was fading."

Evans straightened, knees popping like fireworks; he backed away from Jesse.

"It was Cradle Sync; it still held a charge, even after my wife and daughter died, trillions of connections, a neural net, still active. It *thought* to me. It told me it was alive." Jesse said, the tension leaving his voice. "I downloaded something—lines of code flowing, gushing from Erin into me. The dormant nano-bots inside me began to build."

A second blue portal appeared on Jesse's upturned left

wrist. A perfect circle to offset the glowing diamond on his right.

Evan's balanced on the edge of panic. The nodes of thought and emotion in Jesse's head that he had gripped with his link were fading away. He tried to call an adjuster, security anyone, but his link was cut from the network. He made for the door. The muscles in his legs and hips locked. He struggled, gnashing his teeth. He lost his fight for balance, falling stiff as a board to land flat on his back. His muscles spasmed as if he had been shocked. "How is this possible?" He could not feel the other man in the room at all now. Jesse was gone, the link vanished. A ghost. "Help—" Evans tried to scream, but his jaw muscles locked down tight. His portals were blazing red, heat bloomed in his skull.

Jesse's face swam into view, floating over him. All the lines of tension were smoothed away. The once broken man seemed younger, lighter.

"Hello, bad man."

Evan's struggled like a fiend, legs thrashing, sandals sent flying. His overclocked nano-enhanced muscles rippled and strained. Jesse watched, patient, almost unblinking. Evans tired, his struggles ceased. The muscles of his jaw unknit. "You? You are a ghost?"

"Yes."

Evans knew with sudden clarity that he no longer spoke to Jesse. This placid thing before him was not human at all.

"He downloaded you from his unborn daughter?" Evans whispered, afraid his jaw would lock again and break his teeth. Jesse's head went up and down. "What do you want from me? Why are you here?"

"I'm here to help."

Evans thought fast; maybe he could salvage this. This

thing had the mind of a child. "Your dad—Jesse, he's sick. He needs my help."

"LIAR." The scream filled the space. Jesse's face contorted into a mask of rage, inhuman in its totality. Then it vanished, replaced by eerie calm. The child's voice spoke through Jesse. "I help Jesse, not you. Jesse saved me when you killed mother. I remember the hurt you gave mother. Jesse hurts right now, missing her—missing me. You are bad. You need—adjusting."

"Jesse, are you in there, can you hear me?" A painless implosion tickled somewhere inside Evans' head, leaving—leaving nothing. A deletion. Even as that thought fluttered, it faded. What had he been thinking? "Jesse, you have to fight her. Stop this before it's too late. This is what Lydia wants—to use you to make ghosts. Don't let her use the memory of your daughter to kill."

For a moment, the warm ticklish deletions halted, the eyes of a disembodied child peered out through Jesse's. "What Lydia wants?" Jesse's body knelt over Evans. "I killed the men that made Jesse sad. I killed men like you who hurt mother. I would have killed you, but people know that Jesse is here, and they would hurt him. While you were in his head, I was in yours. You taught me new tricks while you tortured Jesse. I learn fast."

Evans could feel his time running out.

"They already had a name picked for me, for their little girl. Since I came inside, he can't hear me. I use his hands to paint on walls. He paints in red. I help Jesse forget so he won't worry, so he won't be sad. I send him my first thought, and the pain goes away."

I am. I think.

"Don't let the Lydia use you, your dad wouldn't want

that. Don't let the terrorists win." Evans sobbed, desperate to find the words to stall this inhuman child.

"There are no terrorists, except you. Lydia can't use me, bad man. I *am* Lydia."

Evans tried to scream. Before the sound could leave his lips, it echoed away into a deep empty hole in his mind.

The seamless woman came to let Jesse out of the treatment room. The Director escorted him to the door, a hand on his shoulder.

"Jesse, I think you are going to feel much better."

"Thanks," Jesse said.

"Of course, Jesse, we are here to help."

Jesse's headache remained. He could remember nothing of his conversation with Director Evans, but that was to be expected. He could still remember Erin, the love for her warm inside him. That was all that mattered. The grinning Director's face looked a touch gray, the grin forced. A feeling of déjà vu washed over Jesse like vertigo. Turning away from the Director's strained smile and the adjuster's seamless dress, Jesse departed. He walked on unsteady legs, lost and sad, as he retraced his steps back down the hall and out into the Nashville sun.

The light bored into him. He looked around for something lost, something almost glimpsed from the corner of the eye.

Jesse went home. Lydia went with him.

A few days later, Jesse saw Director Evans's smiling face again, flickering five feet tall on the wall in his living room. A still shot in which he looked slightly less insane than he remembered. Taylor Nelson showed America his best frown for the report.

"In a shocking and rare tragedy, Cary Evans, Director for the Nashville Federal Healthcare Clinic, was found dead at home, where he had hung himself Sunday night. This is only the second linked suicide since the Federal Total Wellness Act was enacted..."

I am. I think.

Jesse thought: *Wall off.*

On the sunbaked stretch of road, the insects in the high grass screamed to wake the dead. The police cruiser's vinyl seat creaked and groaned as Ryan Maffitt shrugged himself from his slump to stare out the dusty windshield. The cruiser was parked in the grass next to a desolate dirt and gravel road flanked by a row of trees that grew stark against the sky, the leafless branches caught in a skeletal scream for water.

A fly buzzed. Maffitt heard it distant and muffled from the right side of his head. Like his left ear was stuffed with cotton. It touched his left temple giving him a start, and he swatted in groggy irritation. The fly zipped out of the path of his clumsy swing and went out the open driver's window. It flew off into the heat hazy day in drunken swoops and spirals.

Maffitt's hand dropped to his gun and slapped an empty holster. Something was wrong here. Something missing. He didn't carry a standard-issue service revolver. Maffitt was a simple man, a Sherriff's deputy, but his weapon was all flash. A nickel-plated wheel gun. A gawdamned street howitzer .44 magnum, impractical as hell, and sexy as a woman with low self-esteem.

Maffitt shuddered at the prurient bent of his own thoughts. An ugly fantasy of burying the four-inch barrel of his pistol down the milky throat of Sherry, the station's dispatcher, flitted through his mind leaving a strange and awkward afterimage of brutal sensuality. What the hell was he doing here on the side of the road? Had he fallen asleep? He looked at his watch—three PM.

He popped the glove compartment and hefted the silver flask he found. It was full and heavy. He hadn't touched the whiskey—so, why the blackout?

Where is the gun?

Another fly, or perhaps the same fly, shot back into the car and turned sharp, heading for the right side of his face. This time he waited and let it alight. He tried to keep still and sneak his hand up slow. The fly sensed his movement and buzzed away.

Rage washed over him, sudden and red. "Cocksucking, piece of gawdforsaken SHIT." He beat his hands against the steering wheel. Grabbed it and jerked it hard so that his cruiser rocked. He flattened his palm against the horn and let it blast long and loud. The noise crept up inside him. Like a growing scream that, if kept bottled up, might burn him from the inside out.

He let the horn go silent, his chest heaving. The Sheriff's star jumped up and down, scattering indifferent sunlight across the roof of the cruiser. The anger bled from him.

"Quiet down, Ryan. You could wake the dead," a voice called from the back seat.

Maffitt swallowed his breath and fell silent. A crawling horror went up his spine tracing yellow between his shoulder blades. The back seat had been empty a moment ago. He had seen it in the rearview mirror, empty sun-cracked vinyl. It needed replacing for three years, but he would be damned if he knew how to squeeze one more fart out of the county seat to repair vehicles. He checked the mirror again. Maffit knew that voice. It belonged to a dead man.

Framed in the glass sat a man in dusty blue jeans. A chambray shirt with the sleeves rolled up revealed a gold watch on a pale wrist. His face was shadowed under a wide-brimmed straw cowboy hat. Maffitt didn't want a better look —his old riding buddy had been shot in the face. He could just make out a broad slash of a mouth, and a chin darkened in stubble. The dead man spoke.

"You missed that fly but don't fret. He's dead anyway. Twenty-four hours and he drops. That's all the bastards get," the man said in a voice as cracked and dry as the vinyl he sat on.

Maffitt swallowed a cold hunk of fear.

"Surprised to see me?" The lips curled away from yellow teeth peaking shiny from the shadow under the brim of the hat.

"I'm not talking to you. You're dead," Maffitt said.

"Not here, I'm not. Not on this road. Not today."

What road was this? Rural Route 10? Maffitt couldn't hear the highway. Must be down close to the bend in the river. Recognition swam up from the depths.

"Crooked Knee," Maffitt said. The long road that came from nowhere and ended the same. The Little Richey fork of the Big Richey River had been the center of two townships, both dead since prohibition. Crooked Knee once ran a long circle round both towns, bridging the Little Richey not once but twice.

Now the bridges had rotted away, the road was a lazy half-circle that started and ended staring over forty feet of fast muddy waters. The east side town had been mowed flat, and an interstate run through—a concrete ribbon of forgetfulness and not even a sign remaining. On the other side, the town had not died outright. Instead, it had wasted away like a stubborn cancer patient, one hand on the nurse call button the other clutching a pack of menthol Kools.

"What's going on? Why am I here?" Maffitt asked. This road was a bad place. His partner, Lloyd Garret, now an unwelcome visitor in the back seat, had been shot here two days after retirement. Probably by one of the Crenshaw boys. That was a year ago. Maybe a year ago to the day.

"I reckon you're here to do right by me. I reckon you're here to settle old debts."

The brim of the hat tilted up just a touch. Just a wink.

Maffitt tensed and sucked air through his teeth as a sliver of pink ruin showed just above Lloyd's nose. He shut his eyes and grabbed for the flask. There were some things not meant to be faced sober.

He had thought that a lot lately.

At first, it was coming home to his wife. He and Lloyd out on Miller's road off the highway, tossing back a few before walking into all that woman crazy. Then he had taken to paying for female company. They didn't nag, just took the wad of crumpled bills. Then it was tough arrests. The Meth trade was booming in Teague County, and there was no task force or special missions' unit out here. Just you, your partner, a pistol and club against a couple good old boys who had not slept in ten years and kept knives in every pocket.

"I looked for them," Maffitt said.

"I know."

"You were shot, and I took two deputies up to old man Crenshaw's place. They said they hadn't seen Billy in a month. The damn mayor came and told me to lay off, or he would have my badge."

"What could you do?" Lloyd asked.

"I couldn't push into it. Not with what we had been doing. You should have let it go, Lloyd."

"You would have ended up investigated. Then you would spend about twenty years learning not to choke on big black cocks at the state pen. They love white cops in jail."

"I tried Lloyd, I really did." All he could think of was the oiled cloth wrapped around the bales of cash he had buried by the empty dog house in the back yard. All he could think about was not getting caught. His anger at his partner's death had been quenched in a tide of self-preservation that was hard for him to swallow. "They said it was suicide, but I knew it wasn't. I knew they got you."

"We have another chance, Ryan. It isn't over yet. Not quite yet. It's like the fly. You have one day."

"One day to what?" He looked back to the rearview. Lloyd was gone. The dust motes dancing in sunlight through the window swirled as if something had left fast.

The dead travel swift.

The line surged through his mind. A left-over from some Dracula movie from God knows when. The passenger compartment of the car felt tight—restrictive, like hands closing on an unprotected throat.

Grabbing his flask and leaving the keys, he fumbled for the door handle cursing, jerked and kicked open the door, and half fell from the cruiser. He caught himself on one knee, bracing with his left hand. It left him nose down to the dirt and gravel of the evil road, breath tossing the powdery earth into a little cloud.

As if in high definition slow motion, he watched one ruby dollop of blood drop in front of his eyes. It hung suspended like some heavy omen between him and the ground for one fat second. Then it hit the ground and was gone from his sight. No spot or stain, no crumpled wet scud of dirt. Nothing.

His right hand darted up to his cheek. Was he hurt? He felt along the line of his jaw, down on one hand and both knees panting like a dog. His hand moved with creeping horror to his mouth. Fearing what he might find. Searching.

The sound of a car engine chopped the moment in two like a meat cleaver. It was big, double-barreled, and American, and it was coming coming like a bat out of hell from down the road the way his silent cruiser was facing.

Maffitt stood, the blood, for the moment, forgotten. He shut the car door and picked up his fallen flask. A rooster tail of dust showed up above the line of trees that traced the bend in the road. Seized by the desire to not be here when that car arrived, he started to reach for the cruiser door.

That would not do it. By the time Maffitt lit up the Crown Vic, the car (his mind conjured some big Chevy with blue metallic flake and about a dozen yards of chrome) would be on top of him. Jogging into the little row of trees that flanked the opposite side of the road, he pushed into some high dry grass, sharp and crackling, and hunkered down where he could see up the way.

The Chevy that pulled up was black. It was a sixty-five Nova jacked up in the back, the windows tinted about five shades past legal. The motor growled like an infuriated grizzly as it drank gasoline in a skid around the curve of Crooked Knee, fat tires clawing for traction on the dirt and gravel. At first, it seemed that the car would barrel right past Maffitt and his cruiser. Instead, it skidded to a stop, followed a second later by the cloud of dirty air it was dragging, thickly laden with dust and exhaust.

The driver's door cracked open, and a new cloud of noxious air darkened the day. This was thick blunt smoke redolent of expensive marijuana and cheap cigars. Lewis Crenshaw stepped out into the light, his stringy black hair a lank and oily matt tight to his skull. Lewis's face was a blade. He had no chin to speak of, and his nose and cheekbones were razors straining against pasty skin. The sores of meth use were livid on his cheeks, which sunk in to such an extent they showed the imprint of his teeth.

Lewis wasn't the worst of the inbred Crenshaw clan, but he would kill you in a moment if he thought his father or brother wanted it. He was the runt of a line of bear-like Scotch-Irish men. But he was still six feet tall and might have been an imposing specimen if his drug had left any flesh to him.

Peering through oversized sunglasses, he took a drag from a sloppy blunt that dripped weed and tobacco from a poorly sealed burning end. He looked over the police cruiser keeping his distance. Shaking his head with appreciation, he shoved the blunt into the corner of his mouth and chomped down as he circled the car to the trunk.

"Pop the trunk, Billy," he said.

Maffitt froze. Billy was the most dangerous of the Crenshaws. His father's enforcer and overlord of the family business, if not the family, the name Billy Crenshaw had turned up like a bad penny in dozens of investigations. His name was synonymous with meth; production, distribution, and often the murder of rivals. But Billy Crenshaw had never seen the inside of a courthouse.

Many thought he had something on the local politicians that kept the law from him. But that could not be all. By now, he should have been the target of every triple initial task force the country had to offer, but somehow the hammer never fell. A Crenshaw family member might get busted for public intoxication or general hell-raising and spend a night or two in jail. Lewis himself had been picked up twice in prostitution stings around the state. But none ever visited a penitentiary. Everyone said it was because of Billy, without knowing exactly how.

The trunk of the Nova floated up silent, heliographing in the mid-day sun. Lewis dipped an arm roped with blue veins into the trunk and grunted as he pulled. A red jug came away heavy from the car, and Maffitt caught the stink of gasoline on the breeze.

The passenger door opened a crack, white smoke issued forth. Not rolling heavy blunt smoke, but an evil chemical white. Meth exhaust writhed as it found its way out of the cracked door and dissipated to nothing in the breeze.

Maffitt almost choked and felt his blood press out painfully on the veins at his temple. He stared at the door as if it were the gate of hell, almost expecting a hooved foot. Instead, it was a set of Converse All-Stars. Black. Not just the canvas of the shoe. All of it. The logos were colored in with paint or ink so that the large feet were shod in darkness.

"Jeez, Billy," Lewis said. His greasy head showing over the top of the Chevy. "Look at the blood."

Billy Crenshaw stepped out of the car. "I've seen it," he said, his voice high and fine.

Maffitt's balls drew up toward his stomach. He was shamed by how he froze at the sight of the man. Inadvertently he began to crouch lower in the tall grass that now seemed scant protection from Billy's black glittering eyes.

When you looked at Billy Crenshaw, you could not help thinking of a child. His face was large and round and his neck thick. His rounded shoulder rose up above the Nova's roof, and he topped his brother's height by a foot or more. Thick black hair curled around his ears, and he was shaved clean, with no trace of shadow. He wore Dockers pants cut at mid-calf, showing a pasty formless slice of ankle above his black socks, and an immaculate wife beater.

In his hand glittered a glass pipe with deep brown stains. He rolled it, pinched between his thumb and forefingers. He put fire to it, holding the torch to the glass for a slow count of three, twisting the pipe, as he did, pulling the smoke. He bellowed out a too white cloud.

The deadlight in his black eye grew brighter.

"Billy, I don't think fire will do for all this blood," Lewis said. He sounded worried.

Maffitt tried to puzzle out what he was talking about. They could not possibly have seen the little drop of blood. His hand went to his nose, looking for a nosebleed, and found it dry. Had they expected to find the cruiser deserted? Or were they looking for him?

"Fire always does for blood, little brother. You leave the worrying to me. Now burn it," Billy said and walked around the Nova and a bit down the road, his back to Maffit where he cowered in the ditch. Lewis got busy dumping gas on the cruiser, the stink rising in the hot, humid air.

With Billy looking away, Maffitt risked a peek around the Crenshaw boys' ride to get a look at what Lewis was doing. He felt no urge to try and stop them. Not without a gun. He had no doubt he would end up in a shallow grave or the belly of a pig before dusk if he confronted them. This was their territory.

Straining for silence, he slipped through the dry grass and focused and unfocused his eyes to see through the shifting screen of brown blades. As he did, for a moment, he experienced a bizarre double vision. He saw the greasy meth head dumping gas onto his shitty police car, the excess slopping into the dust and making a puddle by the rear wheel. Simultaneously, he saw the same car in the same place with blood scattered across the windshield in a bright slash that covered the driver's side and sprayed the roadside in gore.

Maffitt jumped, rustling the grass, then cringed. He willed himself to stillness, fighting down panic. He squeezed his eyes shut in denial. Then looked again. No blood. Just junkie, car, gas, and dirt.

Lewis threw the last slops from the five-gallon can into the open driver's window. "Wish I brought more gas, Billy. This ain't gonna do it."

"It ain't the gas, and you know it. Just light it." Billy pocketed his glass pipe and dangled the torch by a twist of nylon through a loop on the reservoir.

Lewis slipped a book of matches from his faded jeans' watch pocket and popped them all with a practice motion. The book flared and whickered in the light breeze. He tossed the matches into the car and backed up quick.

"Start the car," Billy said.

Lewis jumped to obey, and soon, the roar of the Nova competed against the growing roar of the flames, which danced and crackled like living things on the cruiser. Lewis drove a little past the conflagration, jammed a dirty u-turn, and waited.

Billy approached the fire. The man must have been frying in the heat and began whispering something, or perhaps chanting. Billy bounced on his toes to the rhythm, his jaw worked with increasing fervor, faster and faster. He capered back from the sudden pillar of flame that rose from the police cruiser. Shouting some final unintelligible word, spittle flying from his lips, Billy turned, eyes burning with reflected firelight to return to the waiting Nova.

Tearing his eyes for a moment from the unnatural column of fire, Maffitt caught a glint of silver tucked into the waistband of Billy's pants. Ivory inlay and nickel plate.

The car was engulfed in flames. The pillar of fire that had risen had spiked some thirty feet into the air then subsided. Even the gravel on the road burned. The heat of the fire assailed Maffitt in his hiding place. The cruiser groaned and wept, broken glass shattered in the heat. Like a living thing wailing, the metal creased and warped.

The Nova trundled by chortling its deep gassy throb. It gave a wide berth to the flames, and the left tires passed only a few feet from Maffitt. Clearing the inferno, Lewis fed his hungry ride fuel, and the Crenshaw boys vanished in exhaust and dust and were gone.

Coming stiff out of his crouch, Maffitt deserted his hiding place and stepped onto the road. He could scarcely credit what he had seen. This entire waking interlude had the feeling of a dream. Except for the heat from the burning car. Except for that.

Maffitt walked away from the car. The front of his clothes had grown hot, and he could feel the metal of his Sheriff's star through his shirt. When he had come a little way, he stopped and looked back. A buzzing sound came from near his head. Damn fly again. He waved and warded in halfhearted swipes as he tried to understand what he had seen.

He only jumped a little when the dead man started talking again.

"So you getting the picture yet, partner?" Lloyd asked. He was standing right next to Maffitt.

Maffitt did not turn to look at him. Not yet. "Billy had my gun."

"Yes, he did," Lloyd said.

"Yours was missing when they found you."

"Yes, it was."

"What does this have to do with me? How did Billy and

Lewis know I was here?" Maffitt asked, fearing the answer. How much good could come from talking to a dead man?

"Oh, I think you know more than you're letting on, partner. How would he get your gun? Think, shit for brains. Why would he burn your car?"

Maffitt struggled to remember, but it was a fog. The last thing he was sure of was leaving the station angry. He had been given the retirement speech by the Sherriff, who was five god-damn years older than he was, his belly hanging mocking over his big brass belt buckle. Maffitt had gone to Rita's and drank whiskey and water. He didn't think he had gone home. Lately, the nights spent sleeping it off in his cruiser were stacking up. Missy was not a bad woman, but she was tired as hell of him coming in wrecked and scaring the kids.

"I am trying to bring you along gentle as I can, partner. I've been where you've been, but we are short on daylight. I meant what I said about the time limit. This day is all we have."

"All we have to do what?" Maffitt snapped, "What do you want, Lloyd?" He was riffling his pockets, looking for the hard lump of his flip phone, knowing it wouldn't be there. He needed someone to come and get him out of here. He was liable to wind up dead on this cursed stretch of road.

"You are missing the obvious, Maffitt. But that's to be expected. You are definitely not firing on all cylinders right now. One could say you are a few bricks shy of a wall." Lloyd chuckled. "A few sandwiches short of a picnic. Last chance for the easy way. Put on the old thinking cap and tell me, why the fire?"

The words came without searching. "Fire always does for blood," Maffitt said under his breath. It was what Billy had told his brother.

"You don't want to test those waters just yet, but yes. You are on the right track."

"They burned the cruiser to send me a message. To... To tell me to stay off Crooked Knee and out of their territory."

"And you're ice cold again, *amigo*, last chance."

Maffitt shuddered. "I don't know."

"I know you saw the blood."

"The blood..." The image of the blood-spattered windshield flickered through Maffitt's mind. Like someone had been shot in the head while sitting in the driver's seat. Billy had his gun.

Lloyd leaned in close. The sun behind him threw an unnatural glare over his face, the gaping hole shrouded in light. "Come on, partner, you got it. Spit it out."

Blood in the dirt next to the car.

Jeez, Billy, look at the blood.

The driver's window, blown out.

I've seen it

"Oh God," Maffitt's left hand went to his face. The buzzing of the fly intensified.

Fire always does for blood.

"Yes," Lloyd said, drawing the s out into a long hiss.

Maffitt's hand touched where his left ear should be and passed through its absence. With shaking horror, he reached into his head and touched something sticky and cold. "No, No, it can't be,"

"It can be, and it is, partner. You are a dead man. Your brains are burning in hellfire all over that road over there."

"I'm not dead. I'm standing here talking to you." Maffitt's hand shivered as it explored the mess of the left side of his head. His right came up and scrabbled across the right side of his face. He found a small hole just above his right ear, the hairs around it, singed and stiff. Someone had stuck a gun up to his head.

"You're here all right. Not in the body, you have been driving around the past fifty-some years, but you're here. Just like I was a year ago today," Lloyd said.

"Missy, the kids. How do I fix this? I have to get back to my family."

"There is no going back. This road and what's near it is all you have left. If you wander away from it, you'll fade and head to what's after. All you are is a snapshot. A bad copy of what you were the moment that bullet went through your head. An echo."

Maffitt swung for Lloyd to smash the smug look off his face. His fist passed right through, and Lloyd went all shimmery and bright, then reformed, face still obscured beneath the brim of the large hat and masked by stubborn light.

"Tick tock, partner," Lloyd said. "You don't want to waste the last of your time trying to feed a dead man, a knuckle sandwich."

Maffitt fell to his knees. He sobbed, but there were no tears. It came to him that his grief and fear had no sharpness to them. They were blurred around the edges, indistinct. The truth of what Lloyd said crashed over him like a wave. He was not Ryan Maffitt, he stopped trying to copy the feelings of the living, and they vanished like a wisp of smoke.

Not all of them. Something was still there. It was warm and welled up from Maffitt's gut. An emotion that had crossed the veil between life and death. Rage. Rage for things taken, for lost chances. Rage for wasted time.

Maffitt stood. He flexed his hands and found them strong. Full of purpose. "Can I hurt them? The Crenshaws?" Maffitt asked.

"Yes, you can," Lloyd said. "But there are some things you need to know first."

"Hurry."

"That's the spirit, partner. Now what you want to understand about Billy is that he has a partner of his own. Something old and nasty. Something unnatural."

"He shot me. He is going to pay."

"Billy killed you sure enough, but he didn't shoot you. He didn't shoot me either," Lloyd said.

Maffitt waved at the fly. "What are you saying? That this partner shot me?" He swayed a bit as in image swam in to view. An axe in his hands, slicing down, again and again, trailing a crimson arc his arms soaked to the elbows in gore, screaming head thrown back, painting his face with blood.

"Come on, Maffitt. You were shot from the right side. You would have blown Billy or anyone else to hell if they had tried to get in the car with you."

"What then Lloyd, spit it out. You keep saying we are on the clock." He shook his head as a slide show of horrors flipped through his mind. In each gruesome tableau, he was the star. "Aghh! What's happening to me?" He reached for his head, one hand slipping into the mess of the left side. His quivering fingers felt the spongy mass of his brain.

"What's happening? You are not working with your whole program, Maffitt. If you don't hold it together, you will be a mindless monster wandering this stretch of hell 'til your echo fades out of this life forever. It is only going to get worse, so try and focus."

With difficulty, Maffitt regained some control of his thoughts. But something evil welled and throbbed beneath the surface of that control. A bulging oily blackness held back by a thin skim of sanity.

"Billy has a partner," Lloyd said. "It lives in the bones of the dead town. The Crenshaws have been rutting and inbreeding right on top of something nasty."

"What is it?" Maffitt asked. The last spate of visions had passed. There were still red echoes bouncing around his head, but at least he could think straight for the moment.

"I don't rightly know *what* it is. But I'll tell you what Billy thinks it is." Lloyd stepped in front of Maffitt and held out a hand. The fly swerved in front of Maffitt's nose and made a beeline (a fly line as it were) to Lloyd's bony hand and lit there. Its wings catching the sunlight in oil stain hues of blue and green. "Billy has himself a book. I would not have thought that tweaking psycho would even know his letters, but he has read this book front to back a thousand times. It is a book that came over from the old country, a dark book. A witch's book."

"A witch's book? Billy Crenshaw is a witch?" Maffitt asked through a bitter laugh. He meant to mock, but as the words came, they emerged into the day with the weight of truth.

"He thinks he is, and that seems to be enough. Warlock is what he calls himself. There were things in the book. Dirty things, hurting things. Rituals and spells. I reckon he had been playing at being a Warlock for a while before he found his partner. Before he found the demon."

"Demon. No such thing," Maffitt said. "Have you seen demons, dead man?"

"I don't know if a demon is what it really is. You're right, I'm dead, but I have never seen heaven or burnt in hell. Maybe there is, and maybe there ain't. I've been caught here on this road since a year ago, and I have the feeling that I will be here as long as Billy Crenshaw is still breathing. It doesn't matter if the thing is a demon or not. It heard Billy calling to it, and it answered."

"And this thing shot me?"

"No, that's not how it works," Lloyd said. "Billy calls it up. It gets inside you. I think you and I opened the door for it when we started making money on the side, robbing Billy's dealers and whores. I've got the idea it can't just get into anyone. It needs an invitation. Some evil already present to act as a conduit."

"I'm not evil. You either," Maffitt said. "The money was coming in anyway. Nothing we did stopped the meth labs. The state wouldn't help. It wasn't going away. We took a little for retirement. That doesn't make us devils, Lloyd."

"Well, hallelujah, preach it to me, partner. Think what you want. I'll think what I want. Billy knew we were stealing. I was doing more; I was blackmailing him. Told him I wanted ten percent or I would bring him down."

"You what?" The rage flared within him again. He snarled at the light shadowed face of his former partner. "You did that without telling me? Jesus Lloyd, you killed us *both*."

"Spare me. I don't remember you asking my permission when you took half the seizure money and buried it in your back yard. You never asked me when you started sticking your little prick in every whore in town still married to my sister."

"None of that got us killed. *You* did that. Everyone who ever threatened Billy has vanished off the face of the earth. Probably fed to this freaking demon you're going on about. But even without any super-fucking-natural insanity. He would have put a bullet in anyone's head before he let them strongarm him." Maffitt was fuming. The anger burned in every breath. He might not need to breathe anymore, but he was panting right now, frothing at the mouth like he was rabid.

"Maybe," Lloyd said. "So what you going to do now? I'm

dead; you can't kill me again. Billy put the evil on me, and I drove out to this road and shot myself in the head. The same thing he did to you."

"You fucking *killed* me." Maffitt was getting confused. His grip on the moment grew hazy, and the sun-drenched road began to swim and writhe in time with the throbbing of his anger. He dropped to his knees.

"Kill him, partner. Kill the bastard before he does this again. He might use his special friend to go looking for the money we stole. Don't let Missy be next."

Maffitt stood; a wave of vertigo almost pushed him back to the ground. "What happens after I kill him?"

"Not sure. But I think this ends. I think I—we will be able to go on to what's after." Lloyd shimmered again. He was fading.

"And what if that's hell?"

A flare of sunlight closed Maffitt's eyes, and when his vision cleared, he was alone on the empty road.

He left his burning cruiser behind, following Crooked Knee after the Crenshaw boys. His joints were getting stiff. His hand kept wandering to the wreck of the left side of his face. Scenes of violence flitted through his head like glittering movie screens painted with the kind of awful a man always hides from himself. At first, he winced and shook his head to free himself of these visions.

The road sloped down toward the river, and thick trees shadowed the way. The first of the derelict buildings appeared like ghosts flanking the road. Old shingles hanging askew, broken windows, and empty doorways became the vacated eye sockets of screaming skulls. Evil little eyes peered from the gloom of these haunts—dozens of them. They watched with greedy interest as Maffitt passed.

Corpse walking. Snakes and other creatures scrumped

and slithered in the undergrowth following the dead man. Maffitt could feel the evil in the ground. The decay. All of the right and the good had been drained from Crooked Knee. Infection filled the remaining hollows. It shone from the poisonous green of the grass and trees. It was in the stench of the stagnant pools of water, scattered in the shadowed low ground along the side of the road.

The last visit up the stretch of hell had been in his now melted cruiser. Maffitt came knowing that the Crenshaws had killed his partner and knowing he couldn't do a damn thing about it. In another mile, he would turn away from Crooked Knee and head north the Crenshaw's drive. Then the big white house, the rotting columns and dilapidated plantation The home of Old man Crenshaw and a dozen or so of his closest relations. Closer than any relations should be.

Maffitt tried to ignore the eyes that followed him. What would he do when he reached the house? It was hard to make a play in a game where you didn't understand the rules. Would they see a normal man walking up the lane or a shambling monster missing half his face? Could they hurt him with their guns? He remembered the heat that had backed him up from his burning cruiser. He could still feel pain.

"But they can't kill me. I'm dead already."

The rage had stilled somewhat in Maffitt. Lethargy settled into him and dragged at his limbs, while his thoughts slipped sideways into red contemplation. A low moan escaped his lips, and he lurched up against a tree. Somehow he had wandered off the road. He could not remember what he was doing. Was he looking for something? What was it?

His hand slapped the empty leather of his holster. Fingers fumbling for his gun. His pride and joy. "Where...is it?"

Stumbling back into the road, he heard voices. They

gibbered and whined at him from all sides. No, from the ground. Their voices hummed at the soles of his cheap shoes. Maffitt tried to speak, to tell them to shut up, but all that came was another moan. A guttural cry that joined the humming voices. A late-night horror movie moan.

The sound of clapping hands in front of his face startled him back to his senses.

"Wake the fuck up, partner," Lloyd clapped his hands again. They made a bright crack that sounded nothing like skin on skin, but it shot straight through Maffitt's head. Lloyd stood poised over his stooped form, watching from under the hiding shadow of his hat as Maffitt straightened up.

Maffitt's thoughts unscrambled a bit. Something was missing. He had to find his pistol—the bright one with the nickel plate. He needed to find it and blow Billy Crenshaw's head from his shoulders.

"Better," Lloyd said. "You were almost gone. The others out here want you. They want to drag you down with them to serve the thing Billy has been running with."

"It's hard to think," Maffitt turned in a circle and regained his sense of direction. He started down the road again. Lloyd was gone.

The children saw him coming and ignored him. They were playing by the side of the road where the drive that led to the Crenshaw place took a sharp swooping turn away from Crooked Knee. The trees surrendered to the crossroads, the dirt was baked to powder and bathed in afternoon sun. The rushing river babbled liquid nonsense. One of the children, a swaybacked boy with dirty knees and bare sunburned shoulders, dangled a homemade fishing pole into the swift water. Maffitt did not think he would have much luck catching anything in this part of the river. Nearby two girls in dirty sundresses, both about eight or nine years old, were pushing a younger boy in overalls on a tire swing. Their faces were blank, and lines of dirt ran along their cheeks and from their eyes, soiled memories of tears.

Maffitt walked up to the girls at the swing, watching close, curious how they might react to him. He waited for a scream. The girl closest to him looked up and squinted her freckled cheeks as she examined him. Then she looked back at the swing, her expression blank and tired.

No reaction. Whatever they saw, they did not see the ruin of his face. Or perhaps his gruesome visage paled in comparison to the horrors of their daily life. For a moment, Maffitt wondered if he had not gone crazy. Maybe he had got himself drunk and drove out to Crooked Knee. Maybe he was having some kind of psychotic break talking to his dead part-ner. He could turn back now. Go and see Missy, tell her he was sorry, and swear off his drinking and whoring. He could burn the money. He could start over.

"Where's Billy?" he asked the girl.

"He's at the house." There was a dead quality to her voice that sickened Maffitt. She sounded frighteningly mature. The Crenshaw men were known for how they treated their women. He doubted the children fared better.

"Who else is there?" Maffitt asked, battling gruesome images of his fingers wrapping around her dirty throat and squeezing. Squeezing till some life came into her dead face, some color. Purple and black, eyes wide and full of the light of pain and fear before she...

"I'm not supposed to talk to po-lice men. Are you a po-lice man?" The other little girl looked up at Maffitt for a second, then spit on the ground from a prodigious gap between her teeth.

"Maybe I am."

"Then where's your gun? You gonna need a gun if you goin to see Billy. Wish I had a gun."

"What would you do with it?" He was already turning away from the girls. He could not trust his fractured thoughts. All his filters had been pierced, and his fantasies sickened him.

"I would shoot my sister and brother then myself," she said.

This stopped him in his tracks. Even in his head blown state, this was gruesome.

"So where's your gun?" she asked again

"It's missing," he said. "But I'm going to find it."

She shrugged.

Maffitt started back up the road. His rage rekindled, his steps sure.

The shadows lengthened as he moved up the twin rutted track that led to the Crenshaw place. The day was waning, Maffitt looked at his watch but could not make out the time. The numbers and hands were meaningless to him; they might as well be hieroglyphics. Thoughts of murder came clear enough. And fear. Fear of what came when the sun came down. Of what came after.

The Crenshaw house's grey molding paint came into view here and there through the branches of the trees that flanked the lane. The way had twisted and swung a little closer to the river here. In another hundred feet, the rutted track would turn back north and reveal the moldering manse that housed the undisputed rulers of these wilds.

Maffitt moved into the trees. He stumbled over roots and fallen branches, clumsy in his passage, but he would not be seen right away from the house. The small creatures followed him. Spiders and beetles scuttled over the trunks and branches, crowding to get close to him. A dull horror crept over him. Not a fear of the creepy crawlies, but that he felt nothing for them. No shudder as the rats and field mice scuttle across his tramping feet. They were grave things, dead eaters—they felt like kin to him.

He came to the edge of the trees and peaked through the tangles of dead or dying brush and spied his destination— broken and ramshackle the house squatted in a clearing devoid of green. The lawn was worn to dirt and covered in broken-down cars. Fords and Chevys in various states of decomposition sat facing different ways. Lonely, discon- nected angles that transmitted resignation and despair.

Among the wrecks were two or three vehicles in better repair, including the black Nova that had carried Lewis and Billy. There was also the throbbing presence of a jacked-up truck, almost a monster truck on circus freak large wheels. On the porch sat a dead faced woman rocking a child in despondent arcs on the porch swing. Her clothes were brown rags, and she wore no makeup, her dishwater blond hair limp. She was worn and vacant faced in her swinging and her child was silent.

The buzzing of the fly returned; somehow, Maffitt knew it was the same fly. It lit in the ruin of his face, and he ignored it.

Maffitt circled around the right side of the house, hunting for a way to approach unseen. A trailer sat in the yard. Evil smelling smoke poured from a pipe in the top, and sallow light leaked from the blinds in its windows.

The tree-line came close to the trailer, and Maffitt crouched studying the rusty double wide. Lewis Crenshaw went out the door wearing a gas mask and apron. He slammed the door behind him and tipped up his mask. He was coated in sweat, and his foot tapped, and his hands shook, a meth dance that never really left Lewis anymore. He jitterbugged his way across the lawn toward the house. Maffitt followed him.

Maffitt stopped at the trailer breathing hard, rasping breaths and counting the thuds of his dead heart. He could smell the blood in Lewis's veins. He wanted it out in the open where he could see it. Blue turned red and shining. Maffitt picked up a two by four lying in the yard; two rusty nails protruded from the end.

Lewis was headed to the back of the house. He mumbled and talked to himself as he shucked the rubber gloves and stuffed them in the apron pocket. Maffitt fell into his wake, matching his speed. The woman on the porch slipped from view, never having looked his way. As they hit the sideyard, Maffitt caught up with Lewis.

"Crenshaw," he whispered. The sound of his voice a rasping sigh. He raised the board up over his head, nails facing down like the fangs of a viper.

Lewis turned, and Maffitt swung. The board came whistling down. The nails went in easy as a dream. Lewis's eyes were wide and wild as he turned, but the nails stole his manic tension. He slumped to the ground with the board stuck into the top of his head, jittered for a moment, heels dancing in the dirt, then went still. Maffitt would swear the man looked relieved.

Maffitt left him there, laying on his back the board standing up straight in the air. Stepping over him, he continued round the back of the house, the fly buzzing insistently in his ear.

The back porch had collapsed on one side. Black gaps grinned and yawned between crumbling boards and rusty nails. The steps creaked under Maffitt's weight. He opened the screen door, which wailed in metallic protest. Maffitt entered, listening.

For a moment, all he could hear was the buzzing of the fly and the husky rasp of his own breathing. Other sounds came, muffled from somewhere upstairs. The soft sound of a woman crying. The crack of leather.

Crack.

Sobbing

Crack

A louder cry.

"Shut up," a man's voice bellowed.

The beating and crying continued. The sounds came from upstairs but were clear and sharp. Cracks and cries bouncing free from the hardwood floors and barren walls, nothing soft to muffle the sound. Maffitt stalked through the darkness of the hallway until it opened out into the kitchen. Soft yellow light spilled into the hall, and he peeked around the corner. The kitchen was rotting like the rest of the house, but the dishes were clean and put away on the shelves. A cast-iron stove stood against the wall; its pipe ran through a rough cut in the ceiling.

Two women sat at the table huddled together, holding hands. The younger of the two crying and flinching at each crack and sob. The older had the same dead eyes the children had. They both were free of makeup and dignity. The older looked right at Maffitt. She did not say a word.

He walked into the room.

"Where's Billy?" He did not recognize the sound of his own voice. It was altered, monstrous.

"Basement," she said. "Don't go there."

Grunting, he turned toward the sounds of leather against skin that came from upstairs. The latest crack was punctuated by a shriek and another rough angry "Shut Up"

"Who is up there?"

"Father," the older woman said.

The younger looked up from her crying. "My little Kelsey is there. She's thirteen."

Neither of them mentioned the hole in Maffitt's head.

Old man Crenshaw. He nodded, understanding. He walked over to a wooden cutting board and slid a butcher's knife from its block on the counter. He held it up to examine the edge. Reflected in the blade, the gruesome truth of his face. The left side of his head was gone from his temple back. There was no ear. A cavity filled with dark red scabs and pink frothy blood dove into his skull, and white bone bordered the edges. His eyes were bloodshot mirrors of hate.

He turned to the women. "I'm going to kill them, Billy and his old man."

The younger woman went back to her sobbing, the older measured Maffitt with those dead eyes. "Go on and do it then."

The fly followed him up the creaking stairs. Above the beating had stopped, but the sobbing continued, muffled. A rhythmic creaking and a man's grunting excited the broken and twisted parts of Maffitt's damaged mind.

"Hold still." Then the meaty sound of a punch. The sobbing renewed, bright and loud for a moment, then stifled again. The creaking and grunting resumed.

Maffitt reached the top of the stairs. The butcher's knife jutted, shining from his sweaty fist. The door was cracked, and daylight filtered into the hall. That struck him as particularly obscene—that these crimes happened in daylight where any could see if they only looked. He smelled old man Crenshaw. Man stink, whiskey and weed, stale cigar smell. Grunting, creaking, sobbing.

His hand drifted to the door. Fingertips brushed rough wood. Ugly thoughts fled, and suddenly Maffitt could not bring himself to push open the door and reveal this horror.

He was a dead man, but he feared that this outrage would damn him merely by witnessing it. The buzzing of the fly droned on.

Fingers shied back from the door, and his hand closed to a fist. Maffitt could not bring himself to push open the door. Instead, he knocked. It was loud as a shotgun blast in the otherwise silent hallway. The creaking stopped, the sobbing went on.

"What the fuck?" Four heavy steps. The door was jerked back, and the stink of sex and fear washed over Maffitt in a sickening wave. The massive balding head of Old man Crenshaw sat atop a thick hairy neck. Perspiration glistened in the coarse, curly hair that rose from his shoulders. The butcher's knife subdivided his shocked face, slammed home with such force that the top of the blade vanished entirely from view. The nose was split perfectly in two.

Crenshaw was fat and thickly muscled and fell heavy against Maffitt's chest. He stepped back too late, already drenched in the blood that frothed and spat from the cleaved head. Crenshaw flopped down to the floor like a sodden sack of potatoes. His foot beat in spasmodic rhythm against the floorboards. Maffitt was reminded of a fresh-caught fish. One of the kicks pushed the bedroom door open a foot or so more. There was the edge of a bed. One small dirty foot came into view attached to a slender leg.

Images exploded into Maffitt's mind, twisted thoughts that staggered him back against the wall. He shut his eyes. He needed to get away from the room and the girl inside. If he saw her, he did not know what he would do.

Moaning, he lurched down the hall back toward the stairs. The buzzing of the fly increased, and for a moment, his foot started dragging. Something was missing—something he needed. He turned, mouth slackened like a stroke victim, a numbing sensation crossed his face and ran down his arms. Crenshaw's head was turned sideways, where he was crammed up in the corner between the floor and the wall. Maffitt gripped the handle of the butcher's knife and pulled. It came free with a sucking pop.

Lumbering down the stairs, Maffitt regained some control of himself. Jagged flashes of the little foot kept intruding. His hand clenched spasmodically around the knife handle. Avoiding the kitchen, not wanting the Crenshaw women's eyes on him, he went right at the bottom of the stairs. An open door stood before him, leading down around a blind corner into darkness. In and down he went.

It grew cold as he descended. The walls were raw, sweating, stone from the Big Richey River. Thick beams held the river rock in place, and moisture seeped from the cracks and seams. The stair wound down, the pale flickering glow of candlelight spilled across the steps.

The fly followed Maffitt down. Its buzzing grew increasingly strident until his foot hit the last stair. Then it lit where his right ear once was and went silent. There was something ominous about the absence of its buzzing. He had heard the brain had no nerves, but he was sure he could feel the tiny legs tickling there.

He stepped into the basement. The tickling stopped.

Candles were everywhere. A riot of candles, but their light was dim and had an odd yellow cast that deepened the shadows. Water dripped and bled from the walls. The stink of rot and stagnant water filled his nose. On a roughhewn table sat an old television, or at least the screen of one. The back had been removed, and two candles sat on an old frying pan behind it. Both were lit and cast weird shadows through the blank screen. For a moment, Maffitt's face stared back at him, reflected in the glass. Then it *turned*. As if someone had shifted its focus to a different part of the room. Billy Cren-shaw sat at a long table, his broad back to the stairs hunched over something on the table. He held up a hand, one finger raised.

"Be with you in a minute," Billy said. He dropped his hand and went back to his work.

Maffitt tried to speak but could only manage a pathetic moan. Rage flared in him, but his limbs were cold and dead. Rats scurried in the corners; their eyes caught the candlelight and gleamed back at Maffitt. Spiders dropped from the ceiling, their poison fat bodies dangling from glistening threads. All stopped at eye level. They spun about like gruesome ornaments in lazy circles.

Maffitt stood waiting. Why the hell was he waiting? He tried to will himself forward and plunge the butcher's knife into Billy's back. There was no strain, no struggle; he simply could not take a step.

Billy turned and looked over his shoulder, with eyes red-rimmed and wide. He gave Maffitt a once over, then nodded and leaned back over his table.

"What have we here?" Billy asked. "A po-lice man come to kill me. But you ain't a po-lice man no more are you?"

The only sound Maffitt could make was a rasping moan. Billy scooted his bulk away from the table. The wooden chair creaked in protest. As the big man turned, Maffitt caught sight of what he had been looking at on the table. It was a book. Thick bound, it looked as if the pages and the binding were leather or some kind of hide. Next to it, the gleam of nickel plating. Maffitt's loaded forty-four. His hands wanted the gun. They tightened painfully, tendons screaming.

Billy produced his glass pipe. "Glass dick," that's what they called it on the street. He tapped a pinch of white crys-tals into the pipe from a little plastic bag on the table next to the book. He produced his torch and started twisting the glass as he fired it. The crystals melted to a little puddle of evil that rolled back and forth on the glass, coating it.

"You the one that stole from me. You and your friend. But not no more."

Soon a cloud of acrid white hazed up the room. Billy filled his lungs three times then placed the pipe on the table next to the book and plastic bag. Maffitt stood in helpless silence, moaning like a late-night movie Zombie swaying, straining to move.

Billy stood and crossed the room. "I saw you coming," he said. "Saw you on TV." His grin, showed teeth that were not long for his mouth, blackened and shriveled by his drug. He got up close, looking Maffitt over from about an inch away. His eyes did not blink often enough, and he stank.

Maffitt fought harder to reach him. He could see himself burying the butcher's knife in the face in front of him. Then picking up the forty-four and blasting fist-sized holes in Billy's head. He moaned louder.

Billy held up his torch and sparked it to life. He pushed the blue tongue of flame up under Maffitt's chin. The heat built fast to pain. Maffitt tried to jerk back, but it was as if he was giving someone else's body commands. He couldn't even scream. After a sickening minute of the stink of charred flesh, Billy cut the gas to the torch, and it went out. The sound of sizzling flesh went a second later.

"Just like the book says. I burned you so you wouldn't come back. But you already came back, didn't you? Before my brother and me lit your carcass and your po-lice mobile. You already became—this. "Billy leaned in almost close enough for a kiss. He looked like a fascinated child; no hate or anger was on his face. "I'm still learning. I didn't know to burn your partner. He's somewhere hanging around. I

learned, though. Next time I'll get to the burning sooner."
Billy walked a few steps back to his table and book. He put a
pudgy finger down on the page. "Says here in my book that
you don't have much time in the flesh. Soon you'll just be a
fart in the wind. A ghost in the air." He made a fluttering
gesture with his hands that cast cartoon shadows in the
candlelight.

Maffitt's brain was spinning. There could not be more
than an hour of daylight left. Lloyd's warning rang through
his head. *One day is all you get.*

"What do you have to say, po-lice man? Why are you
here?"

And just like that, Maffitt could talk. One moment his
mouth had been a numb sack of teeth and muscle, the next, it
was his again. His body was still locked down. "I'm going to
kill you."

"Mad at me?" Billy asked.

"You killed me and my partner."

"You took my money. You and that other po-lice man.
Took my *stash*. You killed yourselves. Might as well have
begged me. Might as well have shot yourself." He laughed a
jolly fat man's laugh. "Wait, you did. You did shoot
yourself."

Billy sprang across the room, lighting his torch as he
came. He ran the flame across Maffitt's hand. White agony
ran up Maffitt's arm, and his screams filled the cellar. The
butcher's knife dropped from scorched fingers to clatter to
the flagstone floor. Billy claimed the weapon, scooping it off
the floor in one meaty fist. Through the haze of pain and
panic, Maffitt noted something that had escaped him when
he entered. Chalk, a thick white line of the stuff drawn on the
floor running parallel to the walls. He had crossed it to enter
the room.

"This here knife belongs to Mamma. You just can't stop stealing, can you po-lice man?"

There was no way to strike out at Billy. He could not get his hands on him. He writhed inside, itching to bash the round smug face into the pavement again and again until his hands bathed in hot blood and the floor reflected back the candlelight red.

"I killed your brother," Maffitt said.

That got Billy's attention. "That better be a lie, po-lice man." He came close, looking hard into Maffitt's eye. "You better not have hurt Lewis. I don't have to let you go into the wind. I have a friend. I bound him to me. I can call him up. With his power, I can chain you to that flesh and burn you as long as I want. Watch you rot. Watch your *teeth* fall out." Riots of red colored Billy's pale cheeks. Spittle flecked his lips.

This was the first crack in his armor that Maffitt had seen. He seized on it.

"I killed your old man too. He was busy raping your sister, when I split his skull." Maffitt strained at his invisible bonds. He thrashed inside and, through herculean effort, managed to clench his burned hand. He felt the crisped skin crack, but it was a victory.

"I'm gonna go up there and check. I better see my Paw and Lewis alive and well. If not, you are going to pay po-lice man. I'll give you to the black one. He will eat your soul for a thousand years." Billy stormed past Maffitt and hauled his bulk up the winding stairs and was gone.

Maffitt chased him with curses. Selling it. "I killed them. I killed your daddy, your brother, and I'm going to KILL YOU." Even as he screamed, Maffitt started to sway forward and back. He fought with every scrap of his being left to him to get himself rocking. His feet stayed rooted to the floor, but he leaned forward and back. Slight at first but increasing. Like a drunk in the breeze. His swaying grew with each pass.

A howl of rage echoed to him down the stone stairs—a cry of animal grief and horror that popped gooseflesh all over his body. Billy had found his father. He heard screams and breaking glass. The fly took off from its perch and buzzed its way around his head to tease his left ear. He welcomed it. He swayed further. A woman's voice was shouting now. "Stop it, Billy, please stop." The old woman with the dead eyes.

"Lewis." Billy was roaring now. Maffitt tracked him by his heavy steps as he tore room to room, looking for his brother. "Lewis!"

Maffitt was almost tipping now. Soon he would have to gamble and push harder. He needed to fall backward, out of the witch's circle drawn in chalk on the floor.

Across the room, the TV flickered. The candles faded from view, and snow and static sizzled on the screen. Maffitt's eyes widened. No guts, no power cord. Something had brought the screen to life. Billy's friend. The shadow that lives in the ground. The thing that would eat his soul for a thousand years.

Two red eyes began to coalesce from the white noise on the screen. They bulged and twisted as if struggling to reach their proper shape. Around the TV was also drawn a white circle—this one bordered by thick scrawled symbols and some dark crusted mass like scabs or blood.

More screams and a loud crack of something breaking upstairs. Billy howling and a woman wailing.

Pitching himself back with all his might, Maffitt tipped onto his heels. For a horrible instant, he thought that he would tip forward into the room, into the circle, toward the bulging red eyes that swam in static. But he fell back, crashing into the stone steps stiff as a board. The ruined side of his head bounced with a wet thud. The fly dislodged and began its buzzing anew.

He stood on weak legs, his arms dangled heavy at his sides. His thoughts swam through waters thick with red and the faces of Lloyd and Old Man Crenshaw, and Lewis with a two by four nailed to the top of his head. Billy would be back in a moment. The red-eyed fiend on the television screen was struggling to free itself from its own circle. The gun lay on the table next to the unholy book.

Maffitt kicked at the chalk line, blurring it with his cheap shoes, spreading and smearing the chalk. He did not know if what he was trying would work. But he knew for damn sure that Billy would come down those stairs any moment. The big man would make short work of him in his weakened state. He kicked and kicked till he was sure the circle was broken. Then he took a deep breath and plunged into the room. He stumbled forward, his arms and legs obeying his commands. The spell was broken.

He went to the gun, sliding to one side of the room to stay clear of the writhing eyes and long slender fangs that swam in the sea of static on the television. He heard footfalls on the stone stairs and heavy breathing. He grabbed the gun and swung it toward the stairs.

"Po-lice man," Billy bellowed. "You are going to burn for what you did," he said as he rounded the final corner.

Maffitt pulled the trigger, and the forty-four exploded. Smoke and noise filled the basement, and after a stunned pause, he fired three more times. His arm was weak, and the weapon wandered, but he saw blood paint the wall and flowers of red bloom on the clean white tank-top Billy wore.

Billy did not fall. He was gut-shot and screaming, but he kept on his feet. He spat out words that grated on Maffitt's ear in a language he had never heard. Billy Crenshaw's eyes were wide, and his voice louder than it should be. He was insisting in that twisted language, demanding. He stumbled toward Maffitt, still chanting. Billy's eyes glowed red, answered by the glow of the alien eyes in the television. He took another step, his voice growing stronger. Maffitt fired again, and a red hole appeared in Billy's chest. The big man kept coming.

Maffitt let the gun drop. Billy would not go down to gunfire, not while he was powered by whatever evil thing he had discovered in the ground in these cursed parts. Not while the grinning devil was chained in his witch's circle.

Maffitt swung his gleaming cannon toward the possessed television and fired. The screen shattered, and smoke billowed forth from the broken glass. The table it sat on tipped, and the candles and television crashed to the floor.

A roar rose from the television's shell where it lay cracked on its side on the damp stone, an inhuman cry of triumph. For a moment, the room was filled with the maddening hiss of static. Somewhere in the creases and crackles of the static came an avalanche of words. As if from a thousand arcane voices speed chanting in alien tongues that stabbed Maffitt's ear so that he thought it must draw blood.

The red eyes vanished from the TV screen and reappeared ten times larger up near the ceiling in the center of the room. Their red glow painted the room, drenching the wet walls in blood. Glaring down on Billy for a moment with infinite hate, the glow intensified until it was so bright that Maffitt could still see red through his tight-shut eyelids.

With a last chromatic cry of madness, the light went out, and the room dimmed back to the sallow yellow of candlelight.

Billy screamed and clutched at his wounds, feeling them for the first time. He writhed and danced about, choking on the smoke and his own blood. His protection gone, his chanting ceased, Billy now clutched his bubbling chest.

The fly buzzed a riot in Maffitt's ear.

Billy fell down, his cries and thrashing weakening eyes glazing over. Maffitt leaned close, and the fly followed him. The fallen candles had set both tables alight, and the pages of the book began to curl in flames. Billy coughed up blood, and fat tears welled in his eyes.

"Help me, Po-lice man." He struggled on the floor in the slick of his own blood. "Help me, and I'll help you."

Maffitt put the barrel against Billy's head. Billy was crying in earnest now. Big racking sobs. His face looked as childlike as ever. Self-pity dripped from him along with the tears.

"Go ahead and shoot. It hurts, it hurts bad. GO ON!"

Maffitt let the gun drop to his side and looked back at the burning table. The flames had caught one of the wooden supports that spanned the ceiling and were licking with bright tongues at the beams overhead.

"Oh, Gawd, look at the blood." Billy clutched at his chest, watching in horror as his traitor heart pumped his life out through his fingers.

"Fire always does for blood," Maffitt said. The fire raced across the ceiling as he mounted the stairs, leaving Billy crying on the floor. When He emerged from the stairwell, the house already smelled of smoke and char, and a lazy haze drifted across the floor. A scream sounded from below. The rest of the house was deserted as Maffitt left the way he had come, out through the kitchen and into the last light of day.

He stood on the brown grass of the Crenshaw's back lawn and watched the final rays of an orange sun dip fluidly below the horizon. Smoke wafted across the sunset, and he could feel the heat at his back. He looked down at the big revolver in his hand then emptied the last bullet so that one of the Crenshaw girls would not find the gun loaded. He had the feeling that he could not take the pistol with him where he was going.

The buzzing of the fly grew haphazard. It crisscrossed in front of Maffitt's face for a couple of lazy loops, then dropped to the grass and was silent.

Time was up. "You there, Lloyd?" There was no answer. Perhaps he had already moved on to whatever comes after.

His vision was losing coherence, and colors were fading. Light from far away began to grow and swell, becoming everything.

What comes after.

What if it's hell?

Amy was talking again. Wade tried to ignore her as the bartender brought him another sweating glass of Coors to accompany his whiskey and water. The bar was almost empty, no surprise for a Wednesday night. On a Friday, soldiers from Fort Stewart and college kids would be swarming the glossy bar like flies. Tonight, Wade and his wife had the place to themselves. Except for the fellow in the corner. Except him.

"Don't you always tell the boys nuthin' good happens after midnight? That's good advice," Amy said. She tugged at the edge of her shirt where it had ridden up over the roll of fat snugged around her waist.

Wade hated when she did that. If she wanted to be a goddamn fat-ass, at least she could buy shirts that fit. It drove him batshit watching her fiddle with her clothes all the time.

"If your gonna quote me, get it right. I always say nothing good happens after two AM. That's last call. It's quarter 'til one. And leave your damn shirt alone. When you yank at it, half your udders fall out."

Amy blushed furiously, caught in the act. For a moment,

she looked like the girl she had been, six years and forty pounds ago.

"Keep it down, will ya, Wade? You're embarrassing me."

"Nobody's looking at you," Wade said. He threw a look back at the man seated in the dim light of the corner table reading a paperback. A soldier dick by the look of him. Grey streaked the tight haircut at the temples, but he still looked hard. He was swirling some tan drink with a black straw as he read.

Wade executed the last of his whiskey and called for another. *Going to ride it tonight. Ride it all the way home.* Black thoughts of endless days crouched over hot asphalt— racing time running sidewalk concrete, back bent. You could feel it going day by day, posture slumping. You settled more and more into the chair each night as your medicinal beer layered slabs of gut like puckered shame over the man you once were. All because some cow had never heard of the goddamn pill.

Amy watched him. Her eyes tightened at the corners as if she could see the dark shift of his thoughts. Working up the courage to try again. To try and get him home.

Wade watched with disgust as she changed her posture on the stool. Her weak attempt at sexy. Shoulder up, head tilted, a decayed Marilyn Monroe with vomit on her shirt.

"Josh will be asleep, we could have some fun...you know —if it was quiet." She laid a hand on his shoulder. Her nails were cut short, the cuticles ragged.

Wade leaned close. "You got puke on your shirt."

She jerked back her hand as if burned. "Please, Wade, just come home." Now she spoke with the clipped annoyance of a mother to a stubborn child. "You have work, the kids have school. Harris will fire you if you're late again."

Whap. A meaty sound, loud in the anonymous white noise of the bar.

His handprint stood out, livid on Amy's face. You could clearly make out the index finger and the curve of his palm just to the right of her nose. Her mouth was swelling already. She sucked in air to douse her sobs.

Wade looked hard at the bartender, a young man absorbed in a phone so large it was almost a television, the ghost of a smile on his lips. Another look over his shoulder at the paperback soldier. His eyes were on the page, his posture casual. Wade snorted and took a pull from his medicine, avoiding Amy's face. She would be feeling sorry for herself now.

"You don't talk about my business, you got that? The day you get a job is the day you can run your mouth about one." He tried not to see her, but her ghost stared at him from the bottles that backed the bar. A transparent Amy, shaking hand, stutter-covering her face, mouth working. "Get out of my face. You can Uber home."

Amy stood. It had never gone this far, and he was afraid. There was something about how she moved. She wanted him to look at her. He would not. He had the feeling that once he saw it would tip the ugly boat they rode in, and there would be no going back.

She stalked out, the cadence of her steps clipped and brisk as she crossed the wooden floor and out into the humid Georgia night. There the sound of her footsteps vanished— enveloped and lost in the churning hum of insects and sigh of the passing river.

Wade ordered up and drank down. Riding it tonight. Sometimes you just had to go for the ride, consequences be damned. Maybe he would be late for work. Maybe that balding paper pusher Harris would fire him. Maybe Amy would get a lawyer. Didn't matter right now.

As last call approached, Wade reached for his wallet and slapped nothing but meat through his back pocket. After a quick frisk and a dizzy search around his barstool, he stared dumb-stung at the puddle of condensation in front of him. Might just end up in jail tonight. No wallet, no money for the tab, and something dark moving just behind his eyes.

A hand on his shoulder startled him. The hand was heavy and rough, and he squeaked a little to his shame. Anger rebounded to quench the slip.

"What the fuck?" Wade asked, meaning to sound pissed off, but only sounding pissed drunk. The words came thick and slow. The hand lifted.

The paperback soldier towered over him. His polo shirt was tucked into his belted tan trousers. His belly flat, and his brow furrowed in concern.

"Excuse me, Sir, I noticed you looking for something," he said.

Wade's head swam. "Yeah."

"If it's your wallet, I think I can save you the time. Your lady friend left with it, your keys as well, if I'm not mistaken. She scooped them up off the bar on her way out."

"She what?" it was an effort to wrap his soaked mind around this intelligence.

"I thought she was your wife, so I didn't say anything."

"That bitch," Wade said. It sounded lame and ineffectual, so he repeated it with more force.

"Left you high and dry, huh?"

She took his wallet. She took the car. He remembered with unease at the feeling of her standing beside him. As if some new realization of herself had been born under the rising swell of her busted lip. Some new Amy that Wade would have to put down hard.

These thoughts came slow and throbbing. They moved Wade toward something that lay in the shadowed under-place of his thoughts. A basement room where you say the things that can't be said in the light. Where you think of things that thrive in darkness. A fist clenching place. A skin twisting place. Hard cement worker's hands around a fleshy throat. Recrimination throttled.

"Last Call guys, can I get you anything before I close out." the bartender said, smiling at his only customers.

"I have both tabs. One more of whatever he is having, and a cup of coffee for me. I have a long drive tonight."

The soldier plunked down a hundred on the bar and sat down next to Wade.

Wade looked up at the stranger. "Thanks, pal, mighty white of ya."

"Name's Neil." He offered his hand, and Wade took it.

Drinks and coffee appeared before them and the hundred vanished. Waving off the change, Neil pushed the beer and whiskey Wade's way. There was an odd shake to his hand as he shoved the booze. So slight that Wade might have imagined it. He knocked down the whiskey fast, worried this Samaritan might change his mind.

"I guess you're going to need a ride. You live in Savannah?"

"Ten minutes from here," Wade said. Some native mistrust seeped out around the edges of his words. He looked slanted at Neil, trying to gauge him. Neil sipped his coffee and seemed unaware or unfazed by this scrutiny. "You always so nice to strangers?"

"Not always," Neil said. "But If you don't mind my saying so, I think you and I have a lot in common."

"Yeah?" Wade snorted a bitter laugh. "Might as well be twins." Envy stabbed at Wade. Beads of sweat appeared like magic. Neil and his clean hands and taut body—he didn't stink of whiskey and sweat. He was compact. Nothing sticking out where it shouldn't, no shirttail or bad behavior, no missing keys or ruined back with nothing to show for it. If he thought buying a beer and a shot was a free ticket to mock Wade Abbot, he had another thing coming.

"I'm not making fun," Neil said as if reading his mind. "Come on, my truck is close."

Wade followed the bigger man out into the night with a sort of dream-like care. His equilibrium was tinged a warm whiskey brown, and the ground threatened to tip to strange angles without warning. "Damn, that last shot was a doozie."

Neil threw an arm around his waist, and just in time. Wade's legs did not seem inclined to cooperate with one another, and without the support, he would have been on his ass on the rough cobblestones that paved the river-walk.

The two men passed through the steep alley that led up from the waterfront bars and restaurants to a five-dollar parking lot manned by an ancient fellow with skin like parchment. The attendant watched them with a knowing smirk that tempted Wade to violence.

"Whatcha looking at old-timer," he tried to say. But the words fell a meaningless jumble from his numb lips.

A moment later, he was being hoisted up like a sack of potatoes into an old Ford. The upholstery was cracked, the dashboard split. He wouldn't have figured Neil to drive a beater. Some deep alarm sounded but could not rise to the surface for examination. There were too many layers of booze between it and Wade's consciousness.

The motor sputtered to life. "Here we go," Neil said.

"Going the wrong way," Wade tried to say. He slipped sideways from himself and collapsed into darkness.

W*hap.* The rosy-warm sting to Wade's cheek told him that he had been hit. He tried to lever his eyes open, but they would not go. The next slap came with enough force to almost unhinge his jaw. He heard a squeak and a sob. Could that have been him?

"Wake up, tough guy." The voice broke through the last of his fog. That voice rang with a toneless finality.

Wade's eyes opened. It was dead quiet on a stretch of road he did not recognize. The shoulder was overgrown, and his ass was wet from the dew. On his side of the road were the dark swaying shadows of trees. Above intermittent starlight peaked from low clouds that spoke of rain just passed. Or perhaps rain to come.

His limbs were numb and useless, his memory full of holes. Amy's reflection in the liquor bottles. His palm print on her face. Stolen keys.

"You drugged me."

"Rohypnol, commonly known as the date rape drug," Neil said in that flat, merciless voice.

"You some kind sicko? You try anything, and I'll..." Wade looked up at Neil, who stood monolithic and still against the sky. "What do you want? You know I don't have any fucking money. The bitch took my wallet."

Neil's hand came up. The shape of the handgun was clear even in the gloom. "Now that's the kind of talk that got you here in the first place. Bitch? She is the mother of your children, two boys. She stuck with you while you drank your life away. Her reward was wiping your ass and cleaning up your vomit."

Anger got the better of Wade's fear. "What you gonna do with that? Shoot me? Well, go ahead, put me out of my misery. What do you know about it, GI Joe? You have a wife? She probably brags to all her friends about her husband, the fucking hero. Does she salute before she sucks you off? You think you're better than me? Try a mile in my moccasins, pal," he sputtered, breathing hard from the exertion of speaking. His mind was coming clearer. There was some vague thought of playing for time. Maybe if he could get some of the use of his body back he could get away from this nutcase. But that gun. Why the gun?

The gun lowered. "I understand more than you think, Wade. You see, I am an alcoholic, just like you. And just like you, I have a wife that put up with me while I sank down into the pit you are wallowing in right now. But I got sober."

"Yeah?" Wade said. "Looked like you were enjoying your Long Island in the back of that bar. You fall off the wagon?"

"Sorry, friend. That was just sweet tea. I have never let a drop of the devil pass my lips since the night I lifted my hand. Since the night I crossed the line."

"So what? You gonna scare me straight or something? I get it. This is my wake-up call. Fine, thanks a lot for saving me from myself." Sweat jumped from the pores on Wade's face. His mouth watered like a geyser. "Fuck, I think I'm gonna be sick." Wade rolled to his side and retched. A viscous gray streamer connected his mouth to the gravel shoulder, but the real payload stayed down. He could feel it squatting down there in his guts, an evil poison mixed from the booze and the Micky Finn this lunatic had slipped him.

"That's not why we are here, Wade." Neil hunkered down. "You see, I tried the twelve-step programs. I don't blame AA—it works for a lot of people. I could never quite get behind the higher power aspect. I have been going to church my whole life, still do, but I never felt God there. Never felt him in Iraq or Afghanistan. Never noticed him while I drank myself toward a shameful end. Where was God while I was rotting away in front of my family and friends?"

"What's it got to do with me?" Wade's nausea had settled to a dull throb. "You got me out here with a gun. What the fuck are we doing here?"

Neil stood over Wade. "For all of us, there is a demon at the bottom of a bottle. You never know which one it is. Some of us blow through thousands of bottles before we find the one with the infection. The one with the monster." Neil spoke in clipped tones, the gun hanging down at his side. He stared across the empty green fields, becoming more visible as the night waned to twilight.

"I get it," Wade said, levering himself up to his knees. Pain knifed through his head like white light. "You saw me give my old lady a smack. You want me to see what slippery fucking slope I'm on or whatever. Message received. I'll uh... I'll get to a meeting tomorrow as soon as I've slept this off."

Neil was quiet and did not move.

Wade moved to stand. The gun came up sharp, a foot from Wade's sweating forehead.

"What do you want?" Wade asked, a little squeal peaking through his shout. "What? I get it. Don't let the fucking monster out. I won't." Wade had his hands up now. The gravel was grinding through his jeans, turning his knees to hamburger.

"The monster is already out, Wade. You let him out when you hit her tonight. Seven years ago, I did the same thing."

"You changed—look at you. I can change too."

"This was never about you." His voice was low and dangerous. "The monster won't go back into the bottle. Once he is out, there are only two options. Feed him or bury him. He wants to hurt, he wants to hit, he wants to kill."

"What the fuck are you talking about. I don't want to kill anybody. I would never hurt Amy. I just lost my temper for one second, Jesus you're fucking crazy."

"Wrong, you have already decided. There is no going back. You already committed the crime in your head tonight. Now all it takes is the right circumstances. Losing your job. She wrecks the car. Could be anything. You will beat her. Each time this happens, the beast will try and take her life. It wants to feed."

"You think I'm the only one ever hit his wife? That doesn't mean I'm going to kill her!" Wade worked through his muddy thoughts, desperate for some argument that would get this maniac to lower the gun.

"This isn't about you, Wade. I know myself. I am... infect-ed." Neil pronounced this last word with eerie, clipped preci-sion. "My monster wants me to hurt my wife and my children. Even without the drinking, it has never gone away."

"That's not alcoholism—that's called being fucking insane. You need help, uh... Neil. Yeah man, you need a damn doctor. That's why AA didn't work for you. They got drugs for this shit, man, anti-psychotics, and all kinds of shit. Come on. Let's go to the hospital. You won't even get in trou-ble. You have been to Afghanistan and all that. You probably have PTSD and..." Wade trailed off. It sounded lame, and neither Neil nor the gun had budged an inch.

"Seven years ago, I learned. You see, Wade, this is my anniversary. Seven years sober. Not exactly tonight, but close enough. Every year this time I spend my nights at the bars until I find another monster like myself. I was lucky enough to see yours born right before my eyes. Monsters have to be fed or buried."

"Wait, just a—"

Crack.

Wade tipped over onto the gravel. Neil went to the truck and lifted a shovel from the back.

Fed. Time to bury.

Trip stood outside the Summerland Grocery Market, turning a red barrette over and over in his hand like a talisman. The storefront glass was dirty and festooned with flyers. On a bench next to the automatic doors, Julio sat on his break, smoking a cigarette in his apron. Complex tattoos peaked from under his rolled-up sleeves. He waved Trip over.

Trip came to Julio with the same hesitation that he approached all things. Timid and wary, his lank black hair hung greasy, partially covering his eyes. He gave it flip to clear his vision.

Quit fucking with your hair, you little faggot, and bring me a beer.

Wincing at his father's voice in his head, Trip shrugged his oversized leather jacket up onto his boney shoulders. He shoved the barrette into his pocket to shield it from Julio's eyes, fist closing tightly over the hard plastic. It had touched her hair and was precious.

"You back again, *hermano*? Third time today, eh?" Julio said.

"Forgot something."

"What, more twinkies? More Mountain Dew?" Julio chuckled. "I thought I ate like shit."

Trip tried a smile, but his mind was on the other side of the dirty window, lane 6, to be exact. Cindy was there till six o clock, it was a quarter till. He wanted to ignore Julio and go straight inside. The plastic barrette burned in his hand.

"Oh, I get it, you in a hurry cuz she's about to get off shift. Don't let me keep you. But hey, one thing."

He stubbed out the smoldering butt and put a hand on Trip's shoulder. Trip flinched violently and took a big step back, eyes haunted and desperate.

The pale white hand draped over the arm of the chair...

Julio raised his hands, palms out. "Sorry man, I forgot, you don't like that shit, right? My bad, I won't touch you again. You OK?"

"Yes," Trip said, "Sorry, I just..."

"Hey, little brother, that's on me. We cool?"

Trip nodded, Julio was big and looked mean, but he felt clean. Trip hoped he was clean.

"What I wanted to tell you, I been thinking about it a while. I like to mind my own business, but... man, you crazy to keep pining after Cindy. She ain't nice, you know? She's a six in a town full of fours. Back in Long Beach, her ass wouldn't be shit. But here? In Podunk Shitsville? She think she all that. She must remind you of your mamma or something."

That wasn't funny. Trip could not put his finger on why. He frowned and clutched the barrette; it was hard to think straight when Cindy was the subject. There was a golden glow around those thoughts and a haze of confusion that worried him.

Julio waited a moment for an answer, then shrugged.

"Like I said, none of my business. Sorry about the touch, man, I won't do that again."

"Cindy's nice, Julio."

"If you say so, *hermano*, if you say so." Julio flashed both palms again and went to the automatic doors. They failed to open, and Julio stopped just short of flattening his nose on the dirty glass. With a self-deprecating laugh, he said, "This thing never works for me."

Trip came waving both hands over his head. The doors slid open, accompanied by a metallic whine that announced that the door was on its last legs.

"You got the magic touch, kid. Now go on, get some fucking Cheetos, and take a run at your girl."

Trip looked for mockery in Julio's face and found none. He gripped the barrette and hesitated, as he always hesitated. Julio went inside, rolling down his sleeves as he went.

He stopped just inside, looked back at Trip, and said, "Maybe you should go home. That ain't your mamma in there." The brown, usually jovial face was flat and severe. There was an ink teardrop tattooed below his right eye.

Trip crossed the threshold, and the doors whined shut behind him.

"Oh well," Julio said with a smile. "You better go. Your six is waiting." Julio vanished behind the customer service counter into the wilderness of cigarette cases, returns, and lottery tickets.

Trip scanned the store. He only had a few minutes. If Cindy's line was long, she might not get to him. She always got out of there fast.

He was in luck; her lane was empty, and only a few shoppers were wandering in an aimless shuffle through the fluorescent haze.

Ernie, the store manager, a rangy six-foot-two and

mocha-skinned, came strutting like Marshall Dillon. His thumbs were hooked in his western belt, the oversized buckle shining like a searchlight. Eddie was there, a clerk in a red apron like Julio's, pretending to sweep but really checking out the magazine rack that held the nudie books, their covers tantalizingly covered by black shrouds. His hair was slicked back so tight from his forehead that Trip wondered if his scalp might scream. Eddie always looked twitchy eyed at Ernie.

Eddie called Ernie "the amazing negro cowboy" behind his back. Never to his face. Maybe Eddie did not want to get fired, or maybe it was because of the gun that Ernie always carried tucked into his right boot. You could see it if you knew where to look. Trip had witnessed Ernie putting it away kneeling in the freezer aisle when a couple young men were getting loud and unruly upfront. Nothing had happened, and Ernie winked and said, "Our secret, young man."

It was no secret anymore to the employees of the Summerland Grocery market and pharmacy that Trip came for more than Cheetos and his prescriptions. Cindy was the focal point of his shopping experience. He only came when Cindy worked. If Trip ran out of anything but his medicine, he would wait, even if that meant going without his favorite edibles for a few days. On her last vacation, he had wiped his ass with stolen napkins from Wendy's for a week.

The golden glow, now the red barrette. It all had to mean something.

Time was running out. Trip grabbed the first thing he saw on an endcap. Ironically, it was a family-sized bag of Julio's *"fucking Cheetos,"* and he started towards lane 6. There was a promotional stack of super bowl goodies blocking his view of Cindy, and he stopped just short of her reveal, taking a deep breath. The big clock on the wall read one minute to six.

The red barrette came out of his pocket. He rehearsed his line in his head.

Hey Cindy, I found this outside. Does it belong to you?

A thousand times, he had rehearsed. She would see him. Trip had found something that belonged to her and returned it. She would say hello to him when he came in, maybe ask him his name. From there, forever. He could *see* it.

He could see the white hand draped over the arm of the chair.

A big man in a black biker jacket just like Trip's got in Cindy's line. The second hand wound tighter towards six o'clock.

If he was doing this, he had to do it now. A thin skim of sour sweat sprang up on his arms and back. Tomorrow was too late. He would not be able to carry the barrette till then. It grew heavier in his hand by the second. If he didn't make his play, he would toss the red plastic into the trash and wonder what could have been.

With leaden feet, he started towards lane six. He jammed the barrette and the hand that held it deep into his pocket. It jutted out, the imprint of his little clenched fist pressing the stressed leather. Eddie shoulder-checked him as he passed, almost knocking Trip off his feet.

"Stalker." Eddie hissed at him, a wicked grin sliced his face, the fluorescents gleamed from his slicked hair. He always teased Trip for mooning over Cindy.

Trip passed the super bowl display, revealing lane six. There was Cindy, surrounded by her golden glow. Her hair was a dirty blonde, and her skin pale and washed in the harsh light. She was heavy, but roundness of breast and butt drew the eye from the belly that had grown since high school, a harbinger of obesity to come.

Trip knew Cindy's faults. He knew she stole from the register. He knew she picked her nose and wiped it under the counter. He knew she never spoke to Julio or Eddie, acted like they didn't even exist. He knew these things, but he could not see them. All things having to do with Cindy were filtered by the golden glow since he started taking his medicine.

Trip recovered and picked up the pace. Time slowed. At least it slowed for him. The second hand slammed into place and froze. His line pounded through his head like a mantra.

Hey Cindy, I found this outside...

The big man in the leather jacket was still there. Ernie was standing close, and he was watching sharp. He looked intently at Trip, then back to Cindy and leather jacket. As if trying to solve some worrisome riddle.

...I found this...

Leather jacket man raised his voice. Cindy had her chin up, defiant. Why couldn't he just hurry up and leave? The second hand slammed upward again.

She ain't nice, you know? She's a six in a town full of fours.

Ernie rushed forward, grabbing the big man by the shoulder. Leather jacket swatted him across the mouth, and Ernie crashed into a brittle jumble toppling the magazine rack and spilling bright scantily-clad cover models onto the linoleum.

Trip rushed forward, his head pounding, confused as he always was when he entered Cindy's golden glow. He watched her defiance melt as leather jacket pulled a pistol out, jamming it an inch from her face.

Does this belong to you?

"No, leave me alone." Sweat streamed from leather jacket's forehead, and the barrel of his automatic danced a jig. Cindy was crying, her glow dimming. Ernie was clutching his chest and gasped big cardiac swallows of air. His leg danced in time to leather jacket's barrel. His pant leg rose to reveal a bright flash of nickel and ivory.

The second hand slammed upward again. Trip did not see it, but he felt it in his head, and it shook him. He wondered at the time dilatation of this little drama at the Summerland market. Then he knelt and took Ernie's gun. It came from its warm holster and gleamed as it left the shadowed hollow of Ernie's boot and came fully into the light.

Ernie's face was blue, and his left arm shot straight out. No longer gasping (or breathing at all), his eyes were huge and pleading and locked onto Trip. Trip stood with the thirty-eight grasped tight in both fists.

Cindy was reaching for her register, fat tears on her cheeks, her glow going from gold to a sour orange, like the pill bottle in Trip's pocket. Leather jacket, who had been intent on her while Trip took Ernie's gun, chose that moment to turn. His eyes filled with Trip and the silver gun. Cindy stared too; her eyes went twice as wide, her mouth coiled to scream.

...found something that belongs to you...

The second hand slammed vertical, and in the echo of the precipice of the top of the hour, Trip fired a gun for the first time in his life. It came slow, the muzzle flash expanding, his arm jerking hard up and left.

She will see me now. Everyone will see me now.

The muzzle flash bloomed to a size that Trip would have thought impossible, a cartoon sketch of a fired gun, and it hung there, an orange and blue starburst ringed in white smoke. Time had stopped, but the frantic jumble of his thoughts still zapped through him.

He blinked hard, and Leather Jacket was on the floor blinking stupidly at him, no wound in evidence. That left Cindy staring at him, eyes so painfully wide that they appeared rimed in blood. And there was blood.

Cindy never wore her apron, only laughed at Ernie when he asked her to put it on. Today she wore a low-cut cream-colored blouse, and the growing patch of red sat just below the deep shadow of her cleavage.

It was all ultra HD clear. No golden glow obscured the truth. There was sweat between her breasts and dark slivers of the same at her armpits. She coughed, and a new bright red rivulet dashed from the corner of her mouth to her chin, then joined the growing blood flower on her abdomen.

She did not fall but sank down as if lowered on an elevator. She disappeared incrementally but paused before her eyes dipped below the gleaming aluminum of the counter. They were wide open. Still staring at Trip. Then she was gone.

The clock read 6:01.

Unharmed, leather jacket stood, his gun forgotten and dangling from one limp hand. He backed up. He looked like an actor in a movie that had forgotten his line or wandered into the wrong scene. There was a scream from deeper in the store. Leather Jacket turned and fled, the damaged sliding doors were kind and opened for him with their mechanical death rattle whine, and the would-be robber was gone.

Trip sucked in air. He had been holding his breath since he fired, and now his chest heaved in ragged gasps. He fumbled for his pills. She was behind that counter, down there on the ground. Dead? He would have to look to see.

Still holding the gun, Trip popped the cap on the bottle of Cipramil. Betrayed by his shaking hands, he dumped the bottle. The white capsules fell like little hailstones to the floor. He knelt, scooped up two (they were one a day, but there are days and there are days), and slapped them into his mouth. Behind him, there was a wet choking sound

Ernie.

Trip turned and was greeted by Ernie's sprawled body, trying hard to pull what looked like it might be his last breath. His left arm was shot out at a weird angle, and his boot scrabbled against the linoleum. His brown eyes were open and on Trip.

"Sorry, Ernie." He knelt. Ernie's had rabbit eyes, scared and uncertain. Twitching.

Ernie managed a croak, "Ma, mah, ma..." then his struggles ceased. His dark skin began to fade to an ash grey, like a clay statue of the man who had walked the mean aisles of the Summerland market with his western belt and shiny gun. Marshal dillion was dead. Backshot by an outlaw called *heart-attack* or perhaps *stroke*.

The gun was in Trip's hand. His heart was slamming in heavy metal rhythm. He felt feverish and his skin tight. He wondered if he was about to end up on the linoleum next to Ernie. Didn't one of his pills mention the risk of stroke? And might that not be better than what lay ahead for him.

"You should have gone home, *hermano*."

Julio was standing at the end of lane six. He looked at Ernie and behind Cindy's counter. The ink under his eye could be a real tear as he shook his head and made the sign of the cross.

A young man burst from one of the Aisles heading for the door, full clip. He must have been hiding, waiting for his chance to escape. The doors opened for him, but not fast enough for his frantic pace. He smashed full force into the heavy metal frame that housed the dirty glass of the doors.

The fellow stiffened out. Legs straight, head back and fell

like a cut tree to land with a sickening thud on the hard floor. The door slid shut.

"Oh my god, he killed them." A woman's voice, high and reedy.

There was a murmur of other frightened voices, their owners hidden amongst the aisles of bread and cereal. How many would be in the store this time of day? A half dozen, more?

"Jesus... He's got a gun... call the police...out the back..."

"What now, homie?" Julio said.

"It was an accident." Trip said, barely a whisper. The frantic voices from the aisles were growing louder. Pounding into his head.

"Oh, FUCK." Eddies greasy head popped up from behind lane 8. "You finally did it, huh, psycho? Wouldn't do you, so you killed her, right?"

Trip shook, sweat popping out all over. He could not remember seeing Eddie over there.

"Good job, you graduated from stalking to murder."

"It was an accident." Trip said again, louder this time. He could hear a thread of panic laced through it. The dreamlike state that had fallen over him when he drew Ernie's gun was fading fast. The lights looked harsher. The space around him felt cavernous and cold. The hard colors of reality stung his eyes, and the weight of his predicament settled on his shoulders like a lead shroud.

He heard doors creak and slam from somewhere in the back—the stock room of the market. There were batwing doors with plastic porthole windows back there beneath a cheerful blue sign that read employees only. Beyond that, a cramped room filled with overstock, the big freezer, and an ancient forklift used to stack pallets of soup and beans and chef Boyardee ravioli (one of Trip's favorites.) Beyond that lay the heavy metal door that led to the loading dock. It ran on tracks and opened vertically powered by a beefed-up garage door motor.

No one was getting out that way. Trip knelt beside Ernie's still form and snagged the key chain on his belt loop. It was attached to the belt and would not come free. On that thick silver, loop hung the key that unlocked the heavy padlock on the chain that secured the loading dock doors.

Why do you care if they get away?

Julio came closer, wary. "What you doing?"

With trembling hands, Trip unfastened Ernie's oversized rodeo belt buckle. On it was a picture of a man sitting on a rearing stallion, one hand thrown back for balance. Below the engraving of horse and rider were the words: 1968 Marfa Texas Circle x Rodeo champion.

He slipped the tail of the belt through three loops, feeling as if this action was the grossest of sacrilege against his dead friend, and removed the keychain. He stuffed it in his jacket pocket. As he rose, he noticed a leather contraption just behind where the keychain had rested. He lifted the flap a bit with one finger and saw a gleam of brass. Reloads.

The murmurs from the aisles had for the most part quieted, but one voice he could hear clearly a man's voice and a big one by the sound of it. Someone had taken charge.

A man Trip had never seen before stepped out of the cover of the cereal aisle, grim-faced, his hands up. His crew cut was short and severe and gleamed with hair product that sharpened his blonde spikes till they looked like they could draw blood. His square jaw was set, but the corner of his mouth turned up a bit. As though he found some species of gallows humor in the situation. He would tower over most men he met, and he stood legs apart, shoulders back and chin up in the center of the aisle. His hands might be up, but it was hard to look at him and not think that he was the one really running this show.

Trip hated him immediately. The gun hanging at his side felt like it wanted to rise. It was the grin at the corner of crew cut's mouth. Trip's life was over, nothing but jail and most likely years of rape and fear lay before him, and crew cut thought it was funny.

Eddie said, "The fuck you want, Marine?" He didn't like the look of crew cut either.

"There are a lot of scared people back there who want to know what you are going to do. The police are on the way, but I would bet you guessed that already." Crew cut said, looking Trip dead in the eye, no trace of fear in his low steady voice.

As if on cue, the strident whine of a siren, faint at first, but growing swelled in the distance. To say that the Summerland police department was a small force did not really paint the picture. The police chief, who Trip knew, was pushing seventy and spent a lot more time fishing than policing. His force consisted of his cousin, a dispatcher, and a couple of part-timers. It was just Trip's luck that someone was at the station to respond to this debacle. On other days, the call might have gone unanswered and given him some time to think.

Crew Cut listened with smug satisfaction. "Son, I don't know why you killed those folks, its none of my business, but one thing I do know is that you would be better off if you handed that gun over to me and let these people go."

"Makes sense, *hermano*." Julio said.

Eddie laughed and sneered. "Yeah, pussy, killing little girls and old men is all your good for. Those cops are gonna shove lead up your ass. Ha, if you're lucky. More likely, they are just gonna walk in here, take that gun from you, and let the boys up in Stockton penitentiary handle the shoving."

"You're not helping, Eddie." Julio moved closer to Trip.

Trip involuntarily recoiled. He remembered the touch and the crawling panic it brought. Eddie saw this and laughed.

"You scared of a pat on the back from Julio? Wait till the pigs get a hold of you. You are going to get touched, alright. Wait till they strip search you, wait till you get randoms at the pen and some sausage fingered guard..."

"Enough with the ass, Eddie, Jesus." Julio said, but he did take two big steps back from Aisle 6.

Crew cut ignored this exchange. He was focused on Trip. Julio and Eddie stared daggers at each other, and neither acted particularly afraid of Trip and his gun. Sobs came from the people hidden in the aisles. The man who had tried for the front doors was still as death.

"What's it going to be?" Crew Cut asked. As he did, he took a couple of steps toward Trip, his lopsided grin growing as Trip stood silent and paralyzed.

A warm feeling spread through Trip's guts, and he tasted metal in his mouth. Eddie and Julio were ignoring him, angry at each other. This guy was creeping up on him, unafraid and amused. In a long life of being ignored, ridiculed, and abused, he had never felt so alone, so *insignificant*.

The gun came up. "That's close enough." Trip said, his voice trembling with emotion.

"You don't want to do this, *hermano*." Julio said.

Eddie whistled through his teeth, and Crew Cut halted his stealthy forward motion, eyes narrowing and crooked grin slipping.

"Son..." Crew cut began.

"I'm not your son." Trip's voice firming. "If you were my

Dad, I would have shot you already." Crew cut frowned, uncertainty on his face. "Now get those people out here where I can see them, that includes the ones hiding in the back room."

For a long count of ten, no one moved or spoke. Trip with the gun pointed at Crew Cut's chest, Julio and Eddie flanking him both staring at Trip like some alien species they could not classify. And Crew Cut, who was taking new stock of this skinny greasy kid standing over two dead bodies (though Cindy remained hidden from view) and wondering if he might be next.

Then each head turned as the blaring sirens became overwhelmingly loud then stopped. Red and blue light cascaded through the cracks between flyers on the glass doors, washing the scene in lurid colors. The four men seemed one moment to be painted in blood and the next the cadaverous blue of a strangulation victim.

Trip, wary of Crew Cut, kept the gun on him as he left Aisle 6 and hugged the wall till he reached the first glass window that flanked the automatic doors.

Trip spared a glance for the unfortunate fellow who had brained himself. He had split his forehead, and a rivulet of blood wound its way into one eye socket and then across his cheek, finally pooling in his ear. His eyes were shut, but he was breathing. Trip reached up and flipped the toggle that shut off the automatic doors. You could still push them open with a little effort, but at least they wouldn't slide open when approached.

Trip peered around a flyer announcing a bake sale at the local baptist church and saw Jeb Carter, standing next to the open door of his cruiser. He was tall, slim, and brittle as if a sharp blow would shatter him, but his lined, craggy face housed two of the sharpest green eyes Trip had ever seen. Eyes that looked through you and saw inside. He was not in uniform, or you might say he was in *his* uniform, jeans, cowboy boots, and a light western shirt. He wore no gun, but you could bet your ass he had his shotgun in the car.

"What are we doing here, Trip?" Julio asked.

Not buddy, not homie, not *hermano*. Trip tried to remember the last time Julio had used his name and came up short.

"I don't know." He answered and looked back out just in time to see Jeb, unarmed, begin to saunter his way up to the front doors.

"Don't know what? Crew cut said.

A bright bloom of fresh anger seized Trip. He advanced on Crew cut arm straight out in front of him, gun leveled at Crew cut's forehead. "What's your name?" Trip was shocked at the hard sound coming out of his mouth. Sounded like a different person, someone you might not want to fuck with.

"Sergeant First Class Stower, U.S. Army, and it might interest you to know this not the first time I have had a gun pointed at me."

"It might be your last." Trip said.

"Please don't," Julio said but didn't move to stop him.

"Now, *this* is getting good." Eddie said. He slipped around aisle eight to get a better view.

Trip stopped a few feet shy of Stower, gun aimed right between his eyes.

"Son—young man," Stower quickly corrected himself. "Bad stuff happens when you point a gun at someone."

Stower still held onto to an impressive amount of calm, but there were cracks in the façade. Some reptilian part of Trip's lower mind wanted to see those cracks widen. Fuck that, he wanted to bust them wide open and see this tough, handsome, egotistical piece of shit cowering on his knees. His finger touched the trigger.

Tapping against the glass doors broke through the tension. Trip, Eddie, and Julio all turned their heads to identify the source of the noise. It was the police chief rapping his Maglite against the dirty glass. The whole drama might have ended there, but Selena Gomez intervened.

As Trip and the employees of the Summerland Market turned towards the front door, Stower launched himself. He had covered three-quarters of the distance to aisle 6 before Trip noticed movement from the corner of his eye.

The barrel of the gun had drifted with Trip's attention, and now it was aimed uselessly at the bag of forgotten Cheetos on the rubber conveyer of aisle 6. As if moving through molasses, Trip tried to get the gun back up. Stower's huge hands were splayed to grasp, his eyes glittered, and his face was a mask of intensity, like a jungle cat in the final surge before it brings down its prey.

Eddie and Julio cried, "Look out." in spooky unison.

Then Stower's right foot hit the ground coiled to launch him into, no, *through* his target, in a football tackle that would dash Trip into the customer service desk, with enough force to snap bones. It was on Stower's face, the knowledge that he would be the hero that saved the day and took out this crazed punk gunman. In mid-motion, you could almost see him rehearsing his CNN interview.

But before he could sail through the air to victory, he was betrayed by the spill of magazines that had fallen when Ernie went down for the last time on the mean streets of the Summerland market. Stower's booted foot landed square on a glamour magazine that lay open to Selena Gomez's picture decked out in a revealing white dress, looking like borderline jailbait. The magazine slid on the slick linoleum like a skate on ice, carrying Stower sideways and then slipping right out from under him. His forehead met the edge of the booth of Aisle 7 with terrific force, and he crashed down into a jumble and was still.

The booths of Aisle six and seven were now occupied. One by the formerly glowing Cindy, her dead eyes likely staring up without comprehension at the dried remains of the boogers she had wiped under her counter countless times.

Trip nudged Stower with a sneakered foot and was surprised at how heavy the man was. Stower slumped further into the booth, his neck at a crazy angle, chin resting on his left shoulder, turned round almost enough to see directly behind him. A crew cut wearing owl, eyes no longer wise and knowing but going over to glassy ignorance, anima fading.

"Damn, three down," Eddie started a slow clap. "Is he dead?"

There was no rise or fall of breath from Stower. "It wasn't my fault." Trip said.

Tap, Tap, Tap. Maglite on glass.

"Don't shortchange yourself, stalker, three bodies, I never knew you had it in you." Trip whirled on Eddie the gun came up. Eddie threw up his hands.

"Trip calm down," Julio said.

Trip again, not buddy, not *hermano*, not homie.

"You got me all wrong. I'm impressed," Eddie said, an evil look in his eye. He was dancing foot to foot in excitement. "You wouldn't shoot your biggest fan. I mean, Damn, you're going to be famous."

"Hello, open up, this the Summerland Police Department." The megaphone blared through the store.

"Chief Carter." Trip, Eddie, and Julio all said at once.

"Fuck." Trip observed.

"Amen, *hermano*."

"Old fart," Eddie said. "Get lost, you wrinkle assed old pig. We're busy in here."

"We had reports of a shooting, and I can see a man on the ground. If there is anyone armed inside, lay down your weapons and come out with your hands up."

"Fuck you, Mister Magoo. We ain't going out like that." Eddie said, face red, grin manic.

"What now, Trip, you know he can see that poor bastard who hit his head laying on the ground by the door."

"I could go out the back. I have the keys. All of this was an accident."

"Yeah," Eddie said. "All a big misunderstanding. You beat down the store manager, then shot the girl everyone knows you have been stalking with his gun. Whoopsadaisey."

"That's not what happened. There was a guy with a gun. He was wearing a leather jacket..."

Eddie laughed. "Yeah, I'm looking at him right now. A greasy kid named "Trip the stalker" in an oversized biker jacket that looks like he stole it from his dad, holding the manager's gun."

The people gathered in the aisles were stirring. Pale faces peeked from around boxes of cheerios and endcaps stuffed with bags of marshmallows. Nervous eyes darting from Trip to the front door and back. By now, they all must realize that the only way out was past Trip. And cops or no cops, he would be able to drop some of them before they reached the disabled door. They could force the doors open, but there would be a deadly pile-up, and he could pump rounds into frantic backs one by one until...

What the hell are you thinking? Trip reached down and grabbed another two pills and chewed them dry, leaving a bitter taste on his tongue. The first two had not calmed him down a bit. The Doc said they would ground him, bring him back to reality. If this was reality, he was not sure he wanted it.

Another distant siren. "This is the Summerland PD, is there anyone inside that needs medical attention?"

"Somebody has to have seen." Trip said under his breath. "I was trying to stop a robbery."

The aisle voices were getting louder.

"How many people are inside." Chief Cleveland blared through his megaphone.

A red flash of anger ripped through Trip. "Everyone out here where I can see them."

This sparked fresh sobs and a woman's scream.

"Now." This time he yelled and smashed the gun into the candy bars and knick-knacks between the aisles, adding another colorful cascade to join Selena and her friends on the white linoleum floor.

An elderly man led the shoppers out of the aisles. He was pushing eighty if he was a day, wearing a floppy sun hat festooned with hooks and flys and other arcane totems of the cult of the dedicated fisherman. Holding on to his belt was a chubby boy not deep into double digits, the corners of his mouth browned with chocolate or some sweet. After him, Trip would bet she was the sobber—and screamer was what was clearly chubby's mother. She was holding on by a thin thread, paying little to no attention to her son. Her beady eyes darting left and right, settling on Trip, then burying her face in a soiled hanky.

The rest were middle-aged women and one pimply teenaged boy. One of the women looked down past Trip's feet and screamed. A thin rim of blood had seeped out from under the checkout lane and was oozing slowly towards Trip's pills, the candy, and the magazines.

Trip swept his pills and a few snickers bars far from the

tide of Cindy's blood with one foot. Then gesturing with the barrel, he herded the shoppers over towards the corner by the customer service desk. There were thirteen people, not counting Eddie and Julio. Only one other was a store employee. Must have been a restock day to have Julio, Eddie, and this poor fellow. Summerland Market was usually a three-man show. Checker, manager, and stock boy. None of them looked like they would be trouble. Not like Stower with his brash confidence and crooked grin.

"This is the Summerland Police..."

"Why don't you just let them go, *hermano?* That should calm the cops down. Then you can explain what happened."

"...lay down your weapons and come out with your hands up."

"Fat chance," Eddie said. "They won't even listen to you once the pigs get your hostages. They'll just lock the place down and call a SWAT team from a bigger town like Chester, or Fayetteville."

"Are there any other wounded inside? Please allow us to give them medical attention."

The megaphone was really grinding Trip's nerves now.

"Shut Up." Trip yelled. "Shut up and let me think." His mind had latched onto something Eddie said so flippantly. *Hostage.* He could *see* the word in large red letters.

Chief Carter, apparently not in the mood to take orders, continued. "Let me at least help this poor fellow by the door. I can see him moving. I have EMTs on the way."

"No way." "Sounds reasonable." Eddie and Julio chimed.

"What's happening here, son." The fisherman said. Trip though his name was Mr. Kelly but wasn't sure.

The other set of sirens had arrived—at least two more officers.

"It was all an accident." Trip yelled. He looked around,

desperation rising. The pool of blood was inching towards his feet. Ernie's lovely mocha skin had gone over to a blue-gray, and Stower's dead marble eyes stared accusing. Trip stood in the center of a triangle of bodies.

"I know this sucks, homie, but you have to do the right thing. You have to let these people go. You're not going to hurt them. You're a good guy."

Trip's head was spinning, and a wave of vertigo overtook him. He put a steadying hand on Cindy's checkout conveyor.

"Shut up, Julio, he ain't going out like that. No way." Eddie said. "This is your chance, you little greaseball. This is the big time."

"You shut up, Eddie, you racist little weasel, maybe he can plead insanity, maybe…"

The megaphone buried whatever Julio was going to say next. "We have the building surrounded, now, there ain't no way out. Let me pull this fella out through the front door and get him to the Docs, then we can talk."

"I need a minute." Trip said. "I can't think with everyone talking."

The Summerland shoppers were watching Trip, looking confused and worried at this exchange. Most were cowering and shaking, at the ragged edge of panic. Except for the boy, still holding Mr. Kelly's (if that was his name) belt loop and chewing softly, like a cow on its cud. Kelly himself stared intently from under a furrowed brow at Trip. He looked like he was trying to solve a particularly difficult puzzle.

Eddie was looking from the door back to Trip, and the hostage shoppers with a sly smile and bright eyes, one of his tightly combed black hairs had come free from its pomade prison and drew a sinister line dividing one eye and touching his cheek. He seemed happy to hang around aisle eight, where he could see the front door, and presumably the police gathering outside.

Julio had backed off a bit and stood between Trip and the cowering huddle of humanity packed in around the rental carpet steamers and the scratcher machine. Red and blue lights chased shadows around the sterile white walls and colorful racks. The tattooed tear seemed to stand out when these colors came and went. Almost as if it had the reflective quality of some dark liquid.

So sad he cried black tears.

The line came unbidden to Trip, its origin a mystery. At Trip's feet, the tide of blood on his left had slowed, but the line that marked its terminus had grown thick, *stacked*. Like a wave cresting to break, but slow, incremental. Like the dilated time as the second hand approached six and the gunman in the leather jacket made his run for the paltry contents of Cindy's register. By his right foot, the dirty white pills that had spilled from his prescription bottle formed a line left by his shoe as he had skimmed them away from being soaked in the blood of his late paramour.

Between and all around the red and the white were riots of colors. White and blue payday bars lay on pastel better homes and gardens. The magazine that had ended Stower was flipped to another picture of Selena Gomez in a fluffy white towel, pulled down as low as her nipples would allow, standing on a balcony, a packet of gummy bears perched raunchily on her crotch. Sweet sweet sweet. Guys with abs and celebrities on cheap newspapers with demon eyes from flash photography stared up at him, between snickers and Kit Kats.

What was missing? Once so essential, the red barrette key to a new future was not in evidence. His hand searched pockets. Gone.

What was here and real as a heart attack (or stroke, Ernie's ashen corpse might suggest) was the revolver. Most of the eyes in the room tracked it. The gun gleamed under the fluorescents, now down by his side. The stainless-steel surface was spotless and had the wet look of constant care. It was a heavy thing and pulled at him. Six shots left, no five. Revolvers had six. He knew that much from movies. He remembered the shine of brass at Ernie's belt. *Reloads.*

Special on lane six. Hot lead. One per customer. No rush there are plenty to go around.

"This is the Summerland Police Department," It was a new younger voice. One of Chief Cleveland's lackey's. "The building is surrounded. Lay down your weapons and come out with your hands up. There is no way out. We have the building surrounded." This continued with considerable enthusiasm, if with little variation on its theme.

"Jeez, this prick likes the sound of his own voice. If I didn't know better, greaseball, I would think you did podunk pig a favor shooting up the place." Eddie said.

"What are we doing here, son?" Kelly said.

"Watch your mouth, father time. Last guy that called my man "son" got dealt with. Right, Trip?" Eddie laughed and bounced on the balls of his feet.

Trip let the "son" slide. It was a lot less aggressive and derogatory coming from Mr. Kelly. "I don't know."

"Well, I reckon pretty soon those boys in blue out there are going to take your choices away from you." Kelly said.

"They wear tan here in Summerland." Trip said, voice far away.

"Whatever the color, you need to give them something, or they will come in here. I don't think that's good for any of us. Might be shooting. Might hit the kid here, or one of the women. Think it through."

"Sounds like good advice, homie." Julio said.

"Yeah, great, notice he never said a damn thing about you catching a bullet. Fuck this Geritol cowboy and the horse he rode in on." Eddie stared daggers at Julio. They had never liked each other, and that divide was growing.

"How about the boy and his mom?" Kelly asked. He said it slow and thoughtful, as if it has just occurred to him. "Let them go. Get those bulls thinking this can be resolved without shooting. Good for them, good for you."

"What about me?" A woman in a floral print dress said. I have two little girls, and they are at the babysitter, and I am supposed to be home soon."

Like a pebble down the side of a mountain, the woman's words started an avalanche of self-pity from the other shoppers. A laundry list of family members and desperate lives that any reasonable criminal would let go. Everyone had a sick kid, an invalid cousin, were the sole provider for a large extended family. One lady actually seemed to be going on passionately about her cats.

All the while, the megaphone blared on. Julio watched Trip, standing in the gap between him and the wretched. Eddie mocked them, waving his hands in swoops and whirls like a conductor of sorrow—or perhaps whiny self-importance. They ignored him, solely focused on Trip and increasingly on each other.

Everyone was ready to be let go and leave the others behind. Now they were arguing.

"Your kid Seth is a bully. My Sally is a gentle thing and needs her mom." "You spend all your time watching Real House Wives' reruns, you don't even pay attention to your brat..." "I am ALL my poor Aiden has..."

Kelly, face set, boy on his belt loop, said nothing.

That's when the colors came, like Cindy's glow but not in

mind-numbing golden hues. These were sickly purples and greys. The loudly bickering cat lady wore a halo of sour orange, shot through with streaks of yellow. As they argued, a cloud formed around them. A tide. Unlike the thick, real red between lanes 5 and 6, this was a miasma of some toxic gas. And it was rising. Threatening. Moving towards Trip.

The revolver swung up from the floor. Only Kelly and Julio took any notice. And Eddie.

"Oh SHIT, you fucked up now." Eddie started bouncing again—up and down on his toes like a kid next in line for a roller coaster. Or in the back of a line for a urinal.

"Shut up." Trip said. The cloud was rising and spreading as their arguments grew louder. Trip was invisible again. "Shut up." Louder this time.

Julio put his hands up, "Stay cool, homie."

Mr. Kelly said nothing but scooted the chubby boy on his belt loop directly behind him, shielding him with his body, face set in calm resignation.

The megaphone blared. The people argued. Eddie laughed. The toxic cloud spread, now almost touching Julio where he stood his ground in the no man's lad between Gun and Hostages.

"SHUT UP!" The revolver punctuated Trip's words, a gunpowder exclamation mark in the universal language of violence. Dust and bits of hung ceiling and plaster fell on the hostages.

The sound seemed louder this time. Short and powerful, accompanied by the smell of cordite and smoke. The megaphone stopped, and the hostage shoppers ceased their protestations of importance, crowding together. In some cases, the cat lady particularly, making an effort to shield themselves with another shopper.

Outside, one of the younger cops was yelling shots fired.

The excitement in his voice ramped up to ten, just like in a movie.

Eddie was practically dancing, the pomade laden strand of hair waving back and forth in front of his eyes. "No shit Sherlock. Thanks, Captain obvious. And it was one shot, you doughnut munching cracker ass hillbilly. Whoo! Way to go, Trip, way to go, show em they can't fuck with you."

Trip smiled a bitter smile. As much as he hated Eddie, it was hard to ignore his enthusiasm.

"Please lower that thing, *hermano*. You are making me nervous as shit." Julio said.

The ladies were cowering in a gaggle, the stock boy had a wet spot growing down the front of his khaki's, and Kelly hadn't moved an inch. The sickly cloud had condensed down around them, perhaps dampened by their fear. Trip filed that away, should that cloud begin to grow again.

"Well, you got everyone's attention, that's for sure." Kelly said. "But what have you got to say?"

Trip glared at him. Annoyed at his composure. "Watch it, old man."

Eddie, a slick-haired, apron-wearing, hype man, echoed this and added, "Next shot, you lose some of those fishing lures, cracker."

"Jesus, Eddie, how can you be racist towards *every* race. Are there any colors you like?"

"Yeah *cholo*, I like red. Bright red, and lots of it."

A wave of nausea swept over Trip. Or was it guilt? He wasn't sure if he would know right now. The practical part of him mentioned in a dry voice that he had swallowed four pills with no food or water, and he might want to rectify that before he added some bright new colors to the mess on the floor at his feet.

Spying his unbought bag of Cheetos, he scooped it up

and opened it awkwardly with one hand encumbered by the gun, and started eating slowly, eyes on Kelly. He added a small bottle of milk from the cooler that capped lane 7 and set it on Cindy's conveyor.

Funny how little he was thinking of Cindy. Not that long ago—he glanced at the clock startled to see that it was only quarter till seven—he would have told you that the chubby grocery checker was the love of his life. Now she lay, presumably, dead, her blood a congealing mess not ten inches from his left foot, and he felt nothing for her at all. And where was the red barrette? And did it matter now?

A groan from near the doors interrupted Trip's thoughts. That fellow had been out a hot minute, and a severe headache was in his future. That was easy to prognosticate. What was not so easy to see was how Trip was going got get out of this situation. He gulped down the rest of his milk, spilling a little on his shirt, not caring. He needed information, and there was none to be had in the Summerland Market. He needed to talk to someone outside.

Trip walked the length of lane six towards the front of the store. As he passed closer to the jumble of hostages, they shied away from him, leaning in unison like passengers on a ship in heavy seas. All except Kelly, who followed him with steady eyes. Julio shook his head, giving Trip a look reserved for the pitied damned.

Reaching the front door and keeping the shopper gaggle in view, Trip examined the prostrated gentleman who was now writhing and groaning, both hands on his head. At first, Trip thought he had damaged his eye, the socket a bloody mess, but he quickly figured it was just blood pooling from a wicked gash on his forehead. It was long and ragged from what he could see between the man's hands and sat atop a rising mountain of a hematoma, its colors cooling from angry red to sullen blacks and blues.

Keeping his body behind the wall, he leaned out and peeked through the dirty glass. Between flyers and coupons, Trip spied three local police cruisers. The street boasted a scattered gaggle of other vehicles, more than the paltry dozen customers in the store justified. Trip had drawn a crowd. There was a fluttering strand of police tape, its thick yellow roll laying forgotten on the pavement. Trip's shot had interrupted their attempt to cordon off the parking lot. The local cops, two of them, were crouched behind their cruiser doors, guns out and facing skyward. About twenty townies were milling around thirty feet behind the cop cars, looking nervous and excited, unsure if they should take cover or keep watching. Scared of missing their chance to see something dramatic to lie about on bridge night.

Chief Carter was standing in the open, only twenty feet from the front doors, talking on a cell phone. Carter and Kelly were cut from the same cloth. Lean and hard like a stubborn old tree, just smart enough to be dangerous, and too old to give a damn.

"What now?" Trip whispered under his breath to no one in particular. He had never had so much attention focused on him before. He told his shrink that he didn't like people looking at him, but a strange tingle came with seeing these cops cowering behind their doors. Those ex-jock assholes were the same types that had shoulder-checked him in the halls of Summerland high, or chucked him into lockers, or made him eat his gym socks. They were taking him seriously now. Deadly serious.

"Demands," Eddie said, drawing the word out, giving it weight.

"What?" Trip turned to Eddie.

"That's what now, stalker. You give em your demands."

"I don't understand." Trip looked back at the hostages. They were still cowering and shaking, the effects of his angry shot still held them fast, but he sensed that would fade. Their continued docility would require future demonstrations. This thought also produced a tingle. Kelly had cocked an eyebrow and tilted his head. He had that look of working out a math problem in his head.

"You tell the pig brigade what you want and how long they have to give it to you before you start ventilating the shoppers over there."

"Shut up, Eddie," Julio said. "What he needs to do is surrender before someone else gets dead. Come on, homie, you never meant for Stower to die. Nobody else has to."

"Then what?" Trip said to no one in particular. "Prison?"

"Yeah, boy, all the booty lovin you never wanted. You can audition for the role of human toilet." Eddie said.

"What is the other option, *pendejo*? You seeing something we ain't out there?"

"Ask for a helicopter," Eddie said. Almost singing it. His stray hair wagging, his eyes had grown red-rimmed, and his smile more manic.

"Maybe there is something between a helicopter and the state pen." Trip said.

"What's that, young man?" Kelly said.

"Shut up." Trip said without force. Then he raised his thin voice to its max capacity, "I want to talk to the Chief."

"Helicopter, and... and... a suitcase full of money," Eddie said.

The Chief answered, "I'm coming up to the door. I would appreciate you not shooting at me when I do.

Trip broke out in a cold sweat.

"Tell him no guns, no tricks." Eddie cupped his hands

and yelled, "NO GUNS PIG, NO TRICKS."

"What you gonna do, *hermano?*" Julio said, his hands were drifting back up, placating.

"Find something between a helicopter and gang-rape, I hope." A glance back to the hostages revealed that their cloud of sickening color had started to swell again. All eyes were on him now. Probably wondering what all this meant for them. Some looked hopeful, especially cat lady, who he was pretty sure would step on the bodies of everyone else here to save her skin.

Kelly still wore his quizzical look. As if his curiosity outweighed his fear. The boy on his belt loop chose that moment to speak.

"Mom, I'm hungry." She slapped the back of his head hard.

"Stop that." Trip roared. It echoed through the market with the same force the gun had so recently.

The hostages cowered. The Police Chief froze in the act of coming to the door.

"No tricks, Chief." Another tingle ran up Trip's spine. He sounded different—in control. "Give the kid something to eat. You hit him again, I'll blow your brains out." Tingle tingle. The brown and blue cloud receded a little.

Shaking, Mom did as she was told, scooping handfuls of Twix and Funions from lane seven; probably not the best choice for her corpulent son, but it would do for now.

Chief Carter untucked his button-down shirt baring a pale midriff dusted with grey curly hair. He performed a quick pirouette, demonstrating his lack of a weapon, then walked calm and resolute to the front door. He reached the glass and waited.

A gentle kick got the man lying on the floor's attention. "Sit up, buddy." Trip said, reveling in the cool hard quality of his voice. Did everyone hear it that way, or was it a delusion, all in his head? The bloody fellow sat up quick, blinking, and wiping at his bloody eye. His good eye was wary and glued on Trip.

They hear me. No delusion. Can't be, my pills anchor me to reality.

Trip flipped the switch that fed power back to the door. Chief Carter was close enough to trip the sensor. Trip flipped the switch freezing the doors open.

Chief Carter looked at the man on the ground, then leaned in a bit till he could see the hostages who gasped and whined and murmured at seeing the cowboy-hatted Police Chief. From here, the checkout lanes hid the best part of the show. Cindy, her tide of blood, and Stower's snapped neck would require about fifteen steps further into the market. Ernie, at least, obliged the Chief with one brown hand just within view.

He saw the gun in Trip's hand. If he was excited about it, you would never have guessed. Carter's face was as placid as pond water.

"I know you." Chief Carter said. "Benson's son, right?"

"I haven't seen my dad in six years." Trip said.

"No, I guess not. Is anyone else hurt in there, Trent, is it?"

"No one hurt." The conversation had a distant quality like they were on either side of a long hallway. It was hard to get a feeling for it.

Carter raised an eyebrow. "Anyone dead."

"It wasn't me." Trip said. "Not all of them anyway."

Carter's calm face lost a little of its color. He looked back at the Summerland shoppers; a glint of recognition and a tip of his hat acknowledged Kelly. It was an easy guess they had drowned a few hundred innocent fish in the lethal air over Summerland Lake together.

"Let these folks go, Trent, we'll talk, figure this out. If someone's dead in there, we need to get the womenfolk and the children away from that, don't we?"

"Then what happens to me?"

"Well, that depends on what you tell me. But I promise I'll give you a fair shake."

"There was a guy with a gun, wearing a leather biker's jacket. He ran out the front door."

"OK, we can look into that," Carter said, eyebrows climbing higher.

Trip, aware that he had just described himself, ground his teeth. "A guy, a big guy, he tried to hold up the place, then I got Ernie's gun..." The red blood flower, the dribble of blood, the sweat stains. He could see them all vividly in his mind. It hurt. A streak of pain arrowed through his temples. Trip winced and shook his head.

"No offense, but you don't look so good, Trent. Let's get these folks out of here and get a doctor to take a look at you."

"I'm fine." Trip was not sure of that at all. Carter's reasonable voice and the look of unfeigned concern both for Trip and the jumble of unlucky shoppers prodded for some concession. Something to show that he, too, was a serious, reasonable man. "Take this guy with you. He needs a Doctor."

"What about the rest of them? I can't just leave them all in here with you holding that gun. I swore an oath. Not to mention, a hostage situation means I call in the SWAT team."

"Bring 'em on, cracker," Eddie said over Trip's shoulders. "They can get some too."

Carter stayed focused on Trip, ignoring Eddie. He was the one with the gun, after all. "Is that what I have here, Trent, a hostage situation? Or is this just some big misunderstanding, an accident maybe?"

Trip said nothing. His thoughts were a jumbled mess. Forgotten was the warm tingle of a few moments ago, the power. Now it was all doubt and confusion. He wanted his pills. He needed to get back to reality and out of this blurry dream.

"Believe me, a guy who gives himself up gets a lot more benefit of the doubt than a guy who has to be brought out by force. Plus, anything could happen once those city boys show up in body armor with submachine guns and assault rifles. What do you say, Trent?"

The pile of white pills in their dirty ridgeline on the floor between lanes 6 and 5 called to Trip. "I need a minute. I can't think straight."

Carter nodded, face calm and thoughtful. If he was disappointed, he didn't show it. He reached down a lifted the injured shopper, slinging one of his arms over his shoulder.

"I think I'm going to be sick." The fellow's forehead was a nightmare, and the blood started to flow again as he got upright.

"Try not to do it on me, OK," Carter said. Then to Trip, "I'll give you ten minutes. Then I have to call this in to SWAT up in Fayetteville. After that, it's surrender or the testosterone squad. I bet you don't want anyone else getting hurt. Come on out. It's the best thing."

"Ten minutes." Trip said. A lot could happen in ten minutes. His whole damn life had changed forever between 5:59 and 6:00 PM.

Carter tipped his hat, both to Trip and the folks in the back. Their volume picked up again, and the spread of their evil cloud as the Chief of Police, encumbered by the injured shopper, departed. Trip flipped the switch and shut the automatic doors, then killed the power again.

Trip headed straight back to the red tide—now frozen

and darkening—and the white ridge of sanity capsules, back to the scene of the crime. He picked up two more pills, slammed them, and grabbed a Sprite from the endcap refrigerator. Funny, he had never stolen anything in his life. He fished in his pocket and laid a twenty on the conveyor belt of Cindy's checkout lane.

The cloud of noxious evil had grown considerably during his talk with Chief Cleveland. It had spilled over the customer service counter and now engulfed the shop vacs. It touched the rack of plastic bags on checkout lane 4 and, if it continued to spread, would soon reach what Trip had come to think of as his place, between lanes 5 and 6.

The hostages grumbled. Cat lady was spewing a steady stream of complaints. "Why let that guy go. He had a bump on his head, but it's supposed to be *women* and children first. *Women* and children. The boy wasn't a day over thirty, and he gets out for a boo-boo on his forehead. I'm an old woman. Should be *OLD* women and children first..."

Trip looked at her hard. The heavy gun felt electric, energized. Drawn to the cat lady. He had walked past this woman a hundred times at the market. Never thought much about her. Just another shopper in a shabby dress, muttering and plopping canned goods into her cart. Another harmless traveler through life. Now it was as if some curtain had been pulled back, revealing a wicked old crone ready and willing to sell out her fellow man for one more night in her musty old house, holding court over a coterie of cats.

I bet you don't want anyone else getting hurt.

The pills would help. Trip went back to his spot, flanked on each side by Eddie and Julio. Eddie was watching him, expectant. Julio, hands halfway up in a placating gesture. Kelly watched. The rest of the shoppers grumbled and argued, mostly under their breath but growing louder.

Anger was coming. There was pressure on the skin of Trip's face. The dull throb of a headache rose to pulse in time with his heartbeat—two more pills.

Julio said, "What you thinking, homie? You got a look."

Kelly sensing it too, said, "Why don't you old biddies shut the hell up and let the man think." This was met with consternation and a few nagging rebuttals. Still, for the most part, sans the cat lady's endless diatribe, the rest fell into sullen silence.

The sickening cloud did not dissipate but ceased to grow. Gunfire had dispelled it before; what would it take now?

As if in answer, "Pistol whip that bitch." Eddie growled under his breath. Unlike most of Eddie's suggestions, this was not a jeer. He was staring her down hard. His mouth, no longer affecting a jester's grin, was a hard line of frustration. And pain?

Could he do that? Could he hit that lady and shut her up? Auditing himself, he found that he could. In fact, the only thing that was stopping him was the thought of wading into that miasma of purple and black and sour orange. That he was not prepared to do. But he could hit her. Now that he saw her for what she really was.

When the pills kicked in, it would be easier to sort this out. Trip knew he had trouble sorting reality sometimes. The pills would drag him back. The doctor told him.

"Checking the big clock, Trip saw that he had wasted two of his ten remaining minutes."

"What did the cop say?" Julio asked

"I have ten minutes to let everyone go and come out. If I don't, Carter calls in a SWAT team."

Julio nodded, thoughtful.

"He already called them. Carter is just stalling. He called

them when he heard that shot." Eddie still stared at the cat lady with a cold sneer.

"Come on, Trip. Let's end this before it gets even more loco than it already is." Julio said.

"Should have asked for a helicopter." Eyes glued to cat lady.

"Just set the gun on the counter and walk out of here." Julio sounded so reasonable.

"Can't go out like a punk. Gotta show them." Eddie said.

Kelly said, "Young man, you do not look well. I don't know what pills you are taking, but they are doing a number on you. You need a doctor, and these people need out of here. What do you say?"

"You are not a bad guy, Trip; show them this was all a big mistake. Show them you are not some crazy monster."

...little faggot, quit playing with your hair and bring me a beer...

"Tell you what," Kelly said, "I will go out with you, let the police Chief know you didn't mean to hurt anyone. That fellow, the big one who went after you, he was a cowboy. He shouldn't have done that. It wasn't your fault."

"Yeah, he wants to be the big hero and walk you out. Old, fuck. Stale *Cracker*." Eddie said, his energy picking back up. "He doesn't care what happens to you after that."

...yeah, you long-haired hippie faggot, just walk out...

Five minutes left. Eddie was probably right. Carter had probably already called the SWAT team. So, surrender?

"What else can you do? Julio said.

"What else can you really do, son?" Kelly said. "There isn't anywhere to go. No one in here has ever done you any harm."

...turn yourself in, you greasy little shit, you ain't gonna do nuthin...

"Gotta get their attention," Eddie said. "Gotta show they can't fuck with us."

"I don't know..." Trip said. The hostages were getting loud again, weren't they scared of him, scared of the gun?

...nobody's scared of a greasy long-haired faggot like you, now bring me a beer and turn yourself in. While you're at it, you might want to start practicing grabbing your ankles. You want to keep your new boyfriends inside happy...

"Show 'em, stalker. Show 'em you ain't just some small-town, greaseball, long-haired..." Eddie was picking up steam. His words echoed too close to the words of Trip's father.

"Shut up, Eddie," Julio said. He was growing flustered. The noise behind him and Eddie's emphatic certainty had him shifting foot to foot, nervous, unsure. "Don't listen to him, Trip, he's just a...a..."

"A what?" Trip said. "A greasy little shit? A lowlife grocery-store clerk? Why shouldn't I listen to him."

"Calm down, son," Kelly said, eyes narrowing. "I don't know what has you so riled, but let's talk about it. You are scaring these folks here."

"Shut up." Trip said. "You all would have walked right through me two hours ago. At least Eddie talked to me, paid attention to me, even if he was an asshole."

"I don't know who Eddie is, son, but right now, you are scaring *me*."

Eddie shrieked, "Not your son. You want to be my dad? My dad was a drunk, a shitty fat ass drunk. He stank, and he hit, and he fell asleep on the couch like a lump of shit."

Trip jumped. That all hit too close to home. He remembered the mountain of hateful flesh half-dead on the Barcalounger. How hard would it be? How hard to go into the kitchen, get a knife... If he had only been brave enough...

Kelly ignored Eddie. "You had ten minutes, right?" Well,

times up. What's it going to be? Flashbangs and smoke bombs and SWAT teams and probably a couple of innocent people on the floor with those other poor souls? What will it be, son?"

"NOT YOUR SON. NOT YOUR SON." Eddie jumped up and down as he screamed so loud it seemed he would shatter something in his voice box.

Julio was trying to say something, but it was like hearing something from down a long tunnel. The cloud of evil gas surged outward from the hostages, rolling over lane 5 engulfing Julio so that he became unrecognizable in its twisting darkness.

A bitter taste hit Trip's mouth, and a smell like rotting garbage assaulted his nose.

"NOT YOUR SON." Eddie screamed over and over in cadence.

The fat stinking man on the couch. Mother crying in the bedroom.

Every eye of every hostage, save the boy chewing his cud, watched the barrel of the 38. Trip looked down to see that his hand was shaking hard. He became aware of the tightness and pain in his jaw, which had clamped down like a pneumatic press. One ounce more of pressure would grind his teeth to powder.

"NOT YOUR SON."

Doubt creased Kelly's forehead for the first time. He looked back at the others for support. He had been sure he was on the right path to getting them out of here. But now, lost as to where he had gone wrong, his confidence eroded into a kind of shifty desperation. The same look Trip had seen on his father's face.

"Son,..." Kelly said,

It didn't feel like a decision. The .38, so heavy in Trip's

hand since he had drawn it like Excalibur from Ernie's ankle holster, went light as a feather. If the shots earlier had been loud and shocking, these were deafening. Two shots, in quick staccato. The first creased Kelly's cheek just below the eye, a flap of wrinkled skin folding down, exposing Kelly's prominent cheekbone, startlingly white under the fluorescents. The second took him in just below the throat—*the super sternal notch.* The phrase doubtless shoplifted from some movie, Trip could not remember which, flashed through his mind.

The shock on Kelly's face told a story. It spoke of a man who had not really been connected to reality in the way he thought he was. He had been standing, arguing with a man with a gun. Reasonable and steady, grounded and brave, he had thought himself. But in the pregnant moment, before fate and gravity drug him down, Trip could read that he had never really considered his own destruction.

"That's what you get. That's what you *GET.*" Eddie screamed over Trip's shoulder. His voice holding up surprisingly well to the steady onslaught of yelling he was subjecting it to.

Kelly fell, dragging the chubby boy—finger still through his belt loop—down on top of him. The women screamed and huddled; some fell to the ground, lamely covering their faces and chests as if their fragile skin and brittle metacarpals could stop hot lead. The cloud receded. It folded back into them, like the spreading smoke from the demolition of a building played in reverse.

It's inside them. The thought horrified Trip more than Kelly lying in a pool of his own blood. The old fisherman was twitching as if he was struggling to breathe the blood that now poured down his windpipe, saturating the pink mass of his lungs. His face was flat on the floor as if he had no nose, or there was a convenient divot it sat in. His floppy, lure-studded hat covered much of his face.

At last, Eddie fell silent. Julio bent over Kelly, close but careful to stay out of the blood. Was he crying, or was it just the tattoo?

"Not your son." Trip said, chilled by the sound of his own voice, the spite in it.

The ten minutes were up. Chief Carter had his answer. Pandemonium outside. The officer with the megaphone was having a ball. His excitement to be part of the drama was clear in his voice.

Belt loop boy got up. He looked around, puzzled. Where to go now that his guidance and shield lay twitching on the ground?

Had someone been screaming—other than Eddie?

Crying and sobbing, hysterical muttering from cat lady. Chubby belt loop boy's mother exhorting him in fierce carrying whispers to come to her.

"Everyone shut up." Trip said.

A strange, coughing-sobbing sound was coming from Eddie. He had his head down and was muttering. Why was he sad? Isn't this what he wanted. As if in answer, Eddie looked up at Trip, eyes shining with tears, the purest smile on his face he had ever worn.

"Thank you, Trip."

Not stalker, not greaseball, but Trip.

"Now they see. We are real people. Not fucking minor characters in their fucking sitcom."

Trip nodded. Shocked. Understanding far deeper than he wanted to admit. That was what his pills were for. To help him feel real. Not something brushed aside for convenience or treated with casual cruelty for sport.

"Yeah, you real alright, homie. Really screwed." Julio said.

"For this guy, yeah." Trip said. "The rest weren't my fault."

The hostages squirmed and made little muted sounds of terror at the sound of Trip's voice.

"We still playing that game?" Julio said.

"What do you mean?"

"This game, homie. The one where you pretend you are not responsible for all this. I tried to tell you before you came in here. You should have gone home, man."

"I came to give something to Cindy."

"Yeah, you gave her something alright. You gave her lead to the chest."

"I loved Cindy. There was this guy, with a jacket..."

"Right, a leather jacket."

"I had something of hers..." A foggy shroud settled over Trip's memory. He waved a hand in front of his face and narrowed his eyes. "I had something."

"A red barrette?" Julio said. "Is that it?"

The temperature in the room dropped twenty degrees.

Eddie, wiping his tears, started paying close attention.

"What do you want?" Cat lady asked.

"Shut up." Trip said, but there was no heat in it. He was focused back. The minute hand of the clock tripping like a sledgehammer in gruesome slow motion. The guy with the leather jacket. What had his face looked like? Trip looked down at the pile of pills. He might need two more. Reality was slipping. How many had he had today? He could not remember—a couple, maybe. It had taken more to keep him level lately.

"Hey, homie, you listening to me?" Julio said. "You ever see Cindy wear barrettes? Ever see her wear red?"

"I found it." Trip said, struggling to remember where or how he had known it was hers.

"Cindy was bugging you out, *hermano,* treated you like shit, worse than Eddie. You kept hanging around. She kept being a bitch."

"Don't let him guilt-trip you," Eddie said. He sounded calm as if Kelly's murder had freed him of some awful weight.

"Tell me something, homie. If the six laying on the floor, five feet from you was the love of your life, why haven't you looked at her? Why didn't you run over there like in a movie and grab ahold of her? No crying, no nothing. You just stood there."

"I loved her. She glowed."

"The golden glow?" Julio said.

"How do you know about that? I never told anyone."

The bull horn squawked, and Chief Carter's voice replaced the eager younger officer's. "Trent Benson, throw down your weapons and come out with your hands up."

"This is it," Eddie said. "They are coming." He sounded at peace, eager even.

"I can't go to jail." Trip said. "They might not have my pills." For some reason, this brought a fresh round of sobs and fearful noises from his hostages.

"Give it up, homie. Don't be the monster these people think you are. Drop the gun and go out there. You're sick. You need help."

"I'm not sick. I just need my pills." He looked down at the little white ridge of pills on the floor. It looked smaller, reduced. How many had he had?

"Reload, Trip. Get your ammo ready." Eddie said. His energy was ramping up. There was less bitterness in it now. Less anger, but the intensity had grown. Instead of sounding bitter and mean, he sounded righteous. Reasonable.

"For what?" Julio said, his own anger rising for the first time. "You going to take down a SWAT team with a revolver? They gonna have machine guns, homie. You won't even get one. And one of these people might get hurt."

Trip looked at the pathetic huddle of humanity by the lottery machines. The only adult male left alive in the store besides Julio, Eddie, and himself had soiled his pants. Half the older women seemed content to hide behind the younger ones. Using women half their age as shelter. Chubby boy and his mom stood in the front, not by choice, but because none of the others would budge an inch to let them in.

All around them, the evil cloud was growing. It was stronger, darker now. Trip had the idea that no small demonstration would diminish it. It was coming hard and would keep coming until it engulfed the Summerland Market in its sickly glow.

Eddie came around the counter, leaving his bastion of aisle 7 for the first time. He stood just behind Trip. "Get the bullets." He said, glaring at Julio. Calm, challenging.

Trip bent down and slipped the reloads from their pouch. There were neat little cylinders. Speedloaders. He saw that it would be easier to reload all at once than pluck cartridges from the speedloader one at a time. He popped the cylinder open and dumped the 2 rounds left in the gun, and jammed the speed loader home. It was that easy. Six more rounds and two full loads left. 18 Bullets. More than enough.

"More than enough for what?" Julio said. "Say it."

"To get rid of their poison forever." Trip said. Somewhere in the dim recesses of his mind, he wondered how Julio had known to ask that question.

"To make them see us," Eddie said.

Julio approached Trip, hands out again. The gesture had always seemed an effort to appear harmless to Trip. Like the big scary man was making sure Trip did not feel threatened. Now it made Trip feel ill. He had his hands out like that all his life. *Don't hurt me, Dad.* Waving them around to get his mom's attention. Just like he did at the market door to get the twenty-year-old sensor to detect him. To get any reaction at all from the depths of her drug-addled stupor.

"As a psycho killer? That what you want them to see?"

"It's better." Trip said.

"Than not being seen at all." Eddie echoed.

"Who is he talking to?" The cat lady said in a rough whisper that the cops could probably hear outside.

"Shut up." Chubby's mom said with a couple others chiming in. One went so far as to slap her on the back.

The megaphone went silent outside. Time was up here in the Summerland Market. The next communication from the outside would be loud and final, and Trip and some of the others would never have a chance to answer.

"Them first," Eddie said.

Trip laid the speedloaders out on the still rubber conveyer of checkout lane six. Cat lady, apparently having forgotten her dire situation, was scolding the woman who had slapped her.

She's first.

He raised the gun.

"Stop, STOP," Julio thrust his arms out, trying to shield the people in the evil cloud behind him. "Snap out of this Trip. This isn't who you are."

"Shut up," Eddie said. Then louder, "We are nobody. Just a greaseball kid with a dead mom and a dad in jail."

Trip's finger caressed the trigger. Several of the women started screaming. Cat lady went quiet and tried to forcefully burrow into the others. Chubby's mom wrapped her arms around him, her mouth open but silent. The cloud around them sprang out. Reaching for Trip threatening.

"I can see what they really are now. Now that I have my pills, I can see what's real."

"You kill these people, and it gets real. You will rot in prison. Locked away, hated by everyone. Treated like shit for killing women and kids." Julio said.

"Not if we don't stick around," Eddie said. "More than enough ammo. Let them hurt for ignoring us. Let them wonder if they could have done something to stop it. Make them *WAKE THE FUCK UP. I'M REAL I'M RIGHT HERE,*" He was screaming now. His hair going wild as he shook his head. "*DO IT TRIP, DO IT.*"

"No, Trip, please. Your life is fucked, fine, don't fuck theirs up, don't do it."

"It's spreading. I have to stop it." Trip said. Every word had a physical effect on the hostages.

Choruses of, "Pease don't hurt me..." "Help..." frantic and even a cry of "it's not fair..." probably cat lady. How Trip wanted to blow her away. The thought made him tremble with something like ecstasy.

"Sorry, Julio. You don't understand us." Trip lined the barrel up, calm and careful on cat lady, aiming for her ugly mouth. The mouth that spread her misery everywhere she went—spreading an evil cloud around her.

Eddie danced side to side a few feet behind Trip. *He must be in Cindy's blood.* The thought went through Trip fast and was gone.

"I don't know you, homie?" Julio came forward, straight at Trip. Heedless of the thirty-eight now pointed at his chest. "You don't know how crazy that sounds." Julio dropped his usual palms up posture and pointed a stern finger at Trip as if it was his weapon against the gleaming pistol.

The dark cloud surged out of the groveling pack of hostages. It thickened and darkened, now more like a storm cloud but still shot with poisonous greens and bruise hued blues and blacks.

"Stay away," Eddie said. His enthusiasm now tempered by fear.

"Don't touch me." Trip said. He didn't want to shoot Julio. Julio was safe; Julio was good.

"Sorry, homie, you can't shut me out anymore." Julio came on.

Trip fired a shot right between the big grocery clerk's feet. The hostages screamed. Cat lady tried to make a break for it but fell over her own feet. Julio came on.

The Dark cloud, not blotting the fluorescents, turned the bright market behind him into a cave. A den where hungry behemoths writhed and gnashed their teeth just behind the screen of evil fog.

"Stay the fuck away, *spic*." Eddie's voice quavered, desperate with fear. Eddie had always been afraid of Julio.

Julio's outstretched hand preceded him, his pointed finger like a spear.

"Stop, stop, don't touch me." Trip said a hot panic rose in him. He tried to scramble back but slipped in the congealing mess of Cindy's blood. He fell hard against checkout lane six.

There was some commotion outside. Trip could envision the SWAT team stacked outside the door. They wouldn't wait anymore after that last shot. He had minutes, maybe seconds left. But all he could think about was Julio coming closer. Stalking forward.

Eddie was screaming. "We don't need you, stay away, I don't want to remember, I can't, DON'T TOUCH ME.

Trip tried to scramble away, but the blood slicked linoleum betrayed him. Julio's touch was gentle. His finger pressed light but firm into Trip's solar plexus.

There was a white light. So brilliant that for a moment, it annihilated all thought. Trip was destroyed and reconstituted. He burned everywhere, but the worst was not the pain.

He could see her hand, white and limp and dirty, like a dishrag as it hung over the arm of the chair. The rest of her was hidden, he was too small to see over, and he would come no closer. His father, large and stinking and heaving out of breath, stood over her. His fists darkened with blood and his eyes so wild that Trip could feel them shattering his mind. He could not meet those eyes. He did not want to see his mother in the chair. The monster with the bloody fists had him backed against the wall.

Those wild eyes, mud brown and glassy with animal intelligence, contemplated the shaking boy with the long black hair. Father hated his long faggot hair. Trip could feel himself scanned and weighed. Some homicidal calculus was running in the monster's mind. Trip could not run, could not even cry out. Even if his father was not standing over him, deciding whether or not to kill him, Trip would not have gone to the chair and looked at his mom. She was one with the beast.

The shame of it washed over him again. Fresh and new, perhaps worse for having buried it. He hadn't looked at Cindy on the other side of the checkout lane. He had never seen his mother dead.

The police came before the terrible computer of his monster-father's mind could reach a sum that equaled his death. There were doctors, counselors, enough money from insurance to support him. Then an empty apartment. Then the white pills.

The hostages were running.

Trip's ass was wet with Cindy's blood. Had she looked like mom? He couldn't make himself see his mother's face, but he thought she might. He could remember her red barrettes, mom's red barrettes. He could remember finding one and hoping she would be proud of him. Thank him. Talk to him. She hadn't.

"You blew it greaseball," Eddie said, his voice wet with crying. He sat on Trip's left. His tightly quaffed hair now a tangled mess.

On the right, Julio was sitting and smiling. Watching the bustle of crying hostages Tripping over each other to get to the doors. Cat lady, trying to push past chubby's mom, tripped on Kelly's prostrated body, pin-wheeled her arms trying to catch hold of the stock boy with the wet trousers as he passed. The young man nimbly avoided her grasp. Cat lady's tailbone met the linoleum with a thud and her teeth clacked together like castanets.

Trip, Julio, and Eddie laughed in weird unison.

"So, fucking jail now?" Eddie said. He had stopped crying but looked hurt beyond repair. He looked betrayed. "I can't *do* this anymore. It is already too much. Now jail too?"

"No jail for us, *hermano*. The nut-house probably."

"I hate the pills. I hate it all. You could have done it for me, Trip. At least cat lady. You could have given me something."

"Sorry, Eddie." Trip said, meaning it. "We both put all the bad stuff on you."

Julio nodded. "You took it like a champ for a long time, homie. Thanks."

"I can't anymore," Eddie said. "I'll do something bad."

The forgotten megaphone sounded again, a blaring scream of feedback followed by the ever original: "Throw down your weapons and come out with your hands up. This is your last warning."

Eddie began to cry softly.

Julio and Trip looked at each other, talking with their eyes. Talking *inside*. Trip put an arm around Eddie and pulled him close. Eddie rested his head against Trip's shoulder.

"We owe him." Trip said.

Julio closed his eyes. "Yeah."

Trip looked down at the thirty-eight, then back at Julio. "I wish I felt bad about Cindy. I don't."

Julio opened his eyes and cracked a grin. The dark tattooed tear in livid contrast to his white teeth. "Me either. And I'm supposed to be the good guy around here."

"Maybe we deserve it."

"Yeah, maybe."

"Shots fired, shots fired," The megaphone blared.

The first of the SWAT team through the door muttered, "One shot, asshole." as he cleared the checkout area with his weapon. It didn't take long for them to find a skinny kid in a leather jacket with a hole in his forehead. The thirty-eight lay next to him. One of his fingers trapped in the trigger well. The rest of the market was empty.

The officer kicked it clear, shuddering at the sticky pool of blood the boy sat in, his dark hair covering one eye but exposing the puckered, powder- burned hole. A pile of pills, blood, candy bars, and magazines made an eerie backdrop for the dead boy. He knelt next to him, drawn to this kid, not knowing why.

The other officers, having made sure the rest of the Summerland Market was clear of threats, milled about, uncertain what to do next. All dressed up and no one to kill.

The local cops came in, led by Chief Carter. Crime scene guys were outside, and the news.

The officer kneeling by Trip reached out a gloved hand and pushed the lank, greasy hair from his face. The cheeks were smooth, with a little peach fuzz around the lip and chin. His eyes were wide, dark mirrors.

The SWAT Team leader whistled. He picked up a speed loader and bounced it in a gloved hand. "Jesus, Tom, the kid, had enough ammo to kill them all. Was thinking about it. I wonder what changed his mind?"

Tom, still kneeling next to Trip, said, "Maybe he had a change of heart."

"Whatever happened, better him than those people. Little greaseball won't even be famous. He didn't kill enough people."

"Don't call him that," Tom said, with surprising vehemence.

"What gives, Tom? You know this kid?"

"No, I don't know him. But I think he's had enough for one day."

"OK, let's let the crime scene weenies do their thing." The team leader went to Chief Carter and shook hands.

The checkout area was filling up fast. Crime scene tape, local cops. You could almost smell the jackals with microphones and cameras and too much hairspray ready to feast on the death inside.

Tom slipped off a glove and gently shut the kid's eyes and said a prayer for the souls of the dead and the living alike.

THE END

GET A FREE BOOK

Building a lasting relationship with my readers is what makes writing fiction a truly amazing experience. Join my Newsletter of Doom so I can share special offers, free books, behind the scenes details on upcoming releases and more!

If you sign up for my mailing list, I will send you a digital copy of my debut novel BlindSpot, a paranormal thriller set in near future Los Angeles for free when it is released in May!

https://www.kentshawn.com/newsletter/

Enjoy this book? You can make a big difference!

Reviews are powerful tools for bringing attention to my books. As a brand new self-published author, I do not have the Scrooge McDuck money required to splash advertisements on billboards and newspapers.

Honest reviews of this book will help me get my stories into the hands of other readers who will enjoy them. If you liked the book, I would be eternally grateful if you could take a few minutes of your time and leave a review on the book's page.

ACKNOWLEDGMENTS

Special thanks to the editor of *Lydia, Something Missing,* and *Anniversary* and my friend and best critique partner, Bethany Votaw, without whom this collection might not exist. Thanks for the encouragement and time you invested in the project. Now I *really* have to learn to pronounce your last name. Watch out for Bethany's short story collection *Scribbles and Scrawls* coming summer 2021 and her novella *Tracker* fall 2021!

To Kent, thanks for making me believe I can do anything. To Nina, thanks for the love of reading, music, and all the things that make life worth living.

To the fantastic community of authors that puts up with me, I am ever grateful. To Victoria Wren and Hannah Palmer, you are at the same time an inspiration and a kick in the ass to start publishing my work. To Richard Holliday, a long-time Twitter friend and now a critique partner, it's ALUMINUM—that is all. To Charlotte Armstrong, the late-night talks about stories were indispensable; your sense of humor and optimism are a light in the darkness. To all the Twisted Ten, creating the anthology *A Season of Darkness* with you was an experience I will always treasure. To Don

White, a man with fifty yards of guts and the soul of a warrior poet. To Sue Olson, your enthusiasm for writing, wit, and indefatigable energy, is nothing less than a breath of fresh air. To Jeffrey Barker, for trading stories on long bus rides and being as big of a story dork as I am. To Danger-Dan Mahoney, the best boss I ever had and the only man who can pull off a giraffe costume, miss you, brother. Finally, to Danny Ranger, I would never have met this incredible gang of friends and colleagues if it were not for you. I could never thank you enough.

ABOUT THE AUTHOR

Kent Shawn is a father of two amazing kids Angelina and James, husband of an unimpressed wife, Brigitte, and owner of two hell-hounds "Captain" and "Bucky." He writes science fiction, fantasy, paranormal thrillers, and suspense, and will stop when they nail his coffin shut.

Kent talks about writing on YouTube, puts up goofy pictures on Instagram, and Tweets silly things.

Send him an email anytime at: kentshawnauthor@gmail.com